The Garden Beyond Her Infinite Skies

MATTHEW KRESSEL

Aya floated over endless effervescing worlds, seeking anomalies. There were a hundred thousand Farmers of the Branch, but Aya was of the best of them all. Her fields were the healthiest, her realms the most pure. Even the Supervisors said she had an uncanny ability to spot the malignant, when others saw but purity. How she longed to find those sickly realms sprouting in her fields, where the oddest things arose, things not found anywhere else on the Branch. Finding one was enough to make her long workdays worthwhile.

She flew low over her fields. Beneath her, a trillion realms sprouted from the ground, spheres budding spheres. Like fattened wheat, the realms leaned tall in the graviton breeze, their thick fingers grasping for the Expanse, while beneath their knuckled bases, tilled to perfection, lay fertile ground. Alone, Aya expressed herself naturally: a ball of prickling white energy, she scintillated. She searched all day, but did not find one anomaly among countless identical realms.

Perhaps, she thought, *I have destroyed them all.*

Repentance Day was nine days away, when all the Farmer Folk would gather to play games of history. Who could remember all the First Ones? Who could reap the neatest row? They'd join to sing the ancient songs, to shout the chorus to the Tall Ones. "Oh, the endless rows! Oh, such majestic beauty!" And Aya played the games and sang the histories, but only because to refuse meant being shamed by those whom she loved.

If only, she thought, *I could write my own lyrics, what stories I would tell them.*

She sighed a cloud of tau neutrinos and watched them tumble into the Expanse. Pulled by the graviton wind, they were lost in the blue

1

haze. What would it be like, she wondered, to float off with the particles, to visit those strange, far off places? But her courage fled with them, as it always did. She couldn't survive in the Expanse, where the winds blew fierce and terrible. She belonged here, on the branchlet. And she would die here. And that made her saddest of all.

She floated above the realm tips, where the ground appeared flat as she hugged it close. But when she soared high, the branchlet's curve became visible. Far upstalk, the horizon bent into itself and formed a tube. And this tube kinked and split into more tubes farther upstalk. And these split even farther up, until the myriad branchlets vanished in the Expanse's blue haze.

And downstalk, her branchlet joined a greater, which joined one greater, which joined one yet greater, and so on, until endless fathoms below all branchlets merged with the Prime Stalk of Thept, blessed be her endless reaching.

Aya flew as high as she dared in the graviton winds, wishing she could see Thept in her gargantuan glory, but the haze obscured all but the nearest branchlet.

Then she dove between rows of baby realms, where myriad spheres still glowed from their inflationary epochs. Their pastel globes lit the way for her spiraling journey upstalk.

The Eighty Eight Lights had just begun their climb up the Prime Stalk, swathing ghostly green swatches across the sky, so that when Aya reached fields of more ancient realms, the landscape plunged into twilight. But even among these brooding shadows, spudded realms winked spectral diamonds from the countless galaxies whirling within them all.

Tiny treasures, she thought, *are hidden inside all things.*

Treasures like Old Gia, who lived in a deep hollow that had been carved into the branchlet. Gia was once a Farmer like Aya, but after long eons, she had grown tired. And as a reward for her service, the Supervisors had given her this home. Old Gia liked to watch the shadows unfold across the Expanse as the Eighty Eight Lights made their daily climb. She hated to be disturbed.

Aya shrunk herself into a respectful torus, taming her wildest energies, as she entered Gia's hollow.

"Go away!" Gia shouted. A colorful and reactive mess of anti-quarks pooled on the ground before her. "I said, go away!" Fits of radiation spluttered from Gia's body, a pallid and diffuse ball of energy.

"But it's me!" Weak blue light from the opening crawled and died a short way in, so that the rear of the hollow was as black as a dead realm.

"Aya? So it is. I don't sense well anymore, child."

2

CLARKESWORLD

MAY 2015 - ISSUE 104

FICTION

NON-FICTION

Neil Clarke: Publisher/Editor-in-Chief
Sean Wallace: Editor
Kate Baker: Non-Fiction Editor/Podcast Director
Gardner Dozois: Reprint Editor

Clarkesworld Magazine (ISSN: 1937-7843) • Issue 104 • May 2015

© Clarkesworld Magazine, 2015
www.clarkesworldmagazine.com

"No, you don't. I'm no longer a child."

"When you reach my age, Aya, everyone becomes a child." She spat out a thin spray of down quarks that drifted to the floor, sparking as they joined the viscous pool. "What brings you here?"

"I was hoping you'd tell me another story of the First Ones."

"Ah, the young farmer grows lonely again."

"I'm not lonely," Aya said. But she wasn't sure if that was true. Out the opening, bleak shadows reached across the Expanse, vaguely menacing. The silence seemed to choke the space, but she couldn't think of anything meaningful to say that had not already been said, as if she was searching for a language she didn't yet speak.

Gia grumbled and retreated into her hollow, revealing a faintly glowing structure that had been hidden behind her. Packed tightly together in a polyhedral pattern was a collection of lights, each a dim pink sphere, like a cold baby realm. Each held a memory. "Your journal has grown," Aya said.

"My memories," Gia said, "have become like a sky full of dying suns, slowly winking out. This is my bulwark against annihilation."

"May I view one?"

"Never. They are too personal. But I'll describe one to you."

Aya shivered off a muon cloud of excitement as Gia plucked a sphere from her journal and absorbed it into her energy-body. The sphere flickered inside her. "I was so young then, barely weaned off ultraviolet milk! I'd forgotten this day. How could I forget? Mama was so colorful, so free."

"Describe her!" Aya said, unraveling her wildest energies.

"She was very different from today's Rearing Mothers. You'd think her energy-body was untamed, her spectra feral. But that's how we expressed ourselves then, expansive, radiant, wild. Mama took my sisters and me upstalk, all the way to a tip."

"Tell me what it was like!"

Gia paused, shivering as if reliving the memory. "Such a sight! I was terrified, but the tendrils mesmerized me. I was surprised because the tendrils didn't bravely reach for the Expanse as I had thought, but cowered from it, as if the Expanse was…cold."

"Cold?"

"These baby tendrils were cowards, Aya."

Perhaps Old Gia was misremembering. The tendrils held the vanguard against the blue Abyss. Or so the songs went.

Gia continued, "Their fear was unhealthy. Mama told us the branchlet had to be excised before its disease spread. We had come to sever her from Thept. Mama showed us how to focus our energy-bodies into Z-beams. And we helped her to . . . " Gia paused, and shivered. "We cut the diseased branchlet free."

Unexpectedly, she vomited the sphere out. It plopped to the floor in a pool of wild particles.

"Gia? Are you all right?"

Gia dimmed. "I've had enough for today, Aya."

"But what did the tendrils look like? How many were there? What did the—"

The X-rays smacked Aya hard. It was just a flash, all Old Gia could muster, but the blow hurt regardless.

"Sentimental child!" Gia snarled. "Why are you here, dreaming when you should be out farming? Get back to work, you wretched tangle of radiation! Get out!" Gia retreated into her hollow, small and dim, barely recognizable as a living creature among the sea of particle noise.

Aya's body stung where Gia had struck her, but she took the blow without reaction, as all good Farmers were taught to do. The pink sphere lay beneath her, an ancient world that might never be seen again, if Gia had her way. Such a shame to let it wink out like a dying star.

Gia was already dozing, spluttering fitful rays, when Aya snatched the globe and darted out the opening. She sped across her fields and flew until she was sure she wasn't followed. Then she set down between a parade of realms that leaned heavily into the Expanse. Shadows tumbled over the ground as she absorbed Gia's memory sphere into her body.

She felt Gia. She *became* Gia.

Her energy-body danced with excitement at being so far from home. And what love for Mama who sprayed off vivid nebulae as she spun up the branch! Its circumference was so thin that she and her sisters could loop around the branchlet in an instant. The ground sparkled a brilliant blue with the glittering particle dew that dusted the surface. No realms had yet formed here. The branchlet was only just born itself.

Gia dared not take her gaze from the ground, because the hideous blue Expanse surrounded her. She wanted to hide inside Mama's energy-body. All the children did. They begged Mama to return home. But Mama called them cowards and smacked them with harsh rays.

"Look!" Mama said. "Look how the tendrils cower from the Expanse, just as you cower now. Your fear is weakness! You must cut it from yourself!" The children whimpered, and she beat them again until they fell silent.

I'm a coward, Gia thought. *I cannot look!*

Mama showed them how to form beams of Z-particles with their energy-bodies, then started the cut. She ordered the children to join her. It took effort, enormous concentration, but soon a furious beam erupted from Gia. All her bottled up rage and terror and sadness leaped out from her. She and the children cut, and the Expanse flickered with the reflected light.

The beams screeched and wailed. But Gia realized the screams came from the branchlet itself. The tendrils cried as the Z-beams moved through them. The sound sickened her, but she didn't stop until the children had severed it through.

Loose from its mother, the baby branch tumbled into the Expanse, tugged by the graviton breeze. It gave such a wail, and giant Thept quivered beneath her as the tendrils reached back for their mother. But it was too late. The branchlet disappeared into the haze of the endless blue sky.

The memory ended. Sickened by the memory, Aya spat out the pink sphere. In a torrent of particles she tossed it far into the Expanse, wishing the feelings would vanish with it.

For a long time she remained in the field. That horrid screeching . . . Those desperate tendrils, reaching for their mother . . .

If only she'd never experienced Gia's memory. If only she could take it back and forget. But she knew she never would.

Thept, bless her endless reaching, had millions of sisters across the Expanse. The Tall Ones grew out beyond the blue horizon, and countless baby realms were born from their myriad branchlets. And far below, their massive root systems plunged into the great ovum called Yi. Just as the realms arose from Thept's body, so the Tall Ones grew from Yi.

Yi herself was one of sixty four ova gestating inside Delicate Womb, the reproductive organ of Mother Lily, who gloriously blossomed inside the 501-dimensional field, Sky of Skies, who accelerated madly inside the meditating Z-space, Incomprehensible Mind, who lived inside another being who had a billion names and even more descriptions, none of which sufficed to circumscribe it. Always, the smaller grew in the larger, on and on eternally, blessed be the All.

The All was eternally full of noise.

Messages trickled down from above like the particle rains. Most were gibberish to the Farmer Folk. But once in a long while, a message became clear. Some ineffable being had told Incomprehensible Mind, who had told Sky of Skies, who had told Mother Lily, who had told Delicate Womb, who had told Yi, who had told Thept, who had told the

Supervisors, who had told the Farmers, to farm and tend the branchlets where countless realms bubbled up from the surface, to keep them free of disease and entanglement so that Thept's growth might continue forever. That message came eight trillion Great Cycles ago, a great long time, even here.

And so the First Ones had razed and tilled Thept's branches, and through generations they'd uprooted corruption, eradicated disease. They had forced the knotted realms into endless neat rows. It had taken eons and countless prunings, but they'd tamed Thept's wildest tendencies. Now, all was arrayed harmony.

But Aya found no beauty in the monotony. In her youth, Rearing Mother had taken her and her sisters to the Tangle, a knot of branchlets downstalk. The First Ones had left it in place to show what would happen if branchlets were left wild.

Iridescent worms wriggled between massively overbudded realms. Spiky balls of baryonic matter clung to the realm tips, popping to release flashing rainbows of particle spores. Anti-matter spiders of a thousand legs pricked realms with their sharp proboscii and grew fat with sucking. The realms formed hoary palaces, gnarled labyrinths and raveled jungles so thick that even airy neutrinos could only travel but a short way in before hitting something dense and impenetrable. And over all this rolled furious particle storms, bathing the fangled corners with strange, brooding energies.

The Tangle was meant to evoke disgust. It was bizarre, Aya thought, but far from disgusting. For ages she longed to enter those twisted realms and dance its grotesque curves, to explore its vulgar corners and play with those exultant infestations of life. Instead, she was taught to revile it.

She had never told Rearing Mother her true feelings. To express them was to invite a beating, or a furlough inside a dead realm, a place frightfully silent, dark, and cold. And she had never told her sisters either, because they betrayed her to gain Rearing Mother's favor. Instead she found it safer to keep silent. And over time that silence had built up pressure, like a realm ready to burst into existence. It was her greatest fear that she could not contain it once it was born.

But Gia's memory gave energy to that silence, threatening to give it form. Aya dreamed often of that severed branch. While flying over her fields she thought she heard echoes of its ancient screams coming from out in the deep.

She was floating low over her twilit, ancient realms one morning when she found an anomaly. She gasped a bubble of charmed quarks. Here, growing among dark arrays, a dim realm curved back on itself, a hooked finger cowering from the Expanse. Or perhaps it turned inward to consider its own curious arising. But this was anathema. To grow inward, a sin. This disease had to be obliterated. A tight beam of Z-particles would do it, would reduce this gloriously wrong realm to a scintillating snow of ash, fertilizer for unborn worlds.

Instead, she peered inside.

Hundreds of billions of galaxies aligned themselves in fine, shining filaments like hoar frost across the hooked realm of 10-space. A tenuous galactic cluster huddled on a filament edge. And inside this cluster, a galaxy furiously twirled. And in this galaxy, a giant red sun hurtled through the dark. And around this sun raced a green planet. And on this planet a purple and white quadruped leaped through a dense forest.

More softly than a falling leaf, the animal tiptoed down to a narrow stream. Its head was long and sleek, its gray horns branching like a miniscule Thept. A breeze trickled through the trees as the quadruped sipped its fill, then gazed up at the orange sky to wonder at the coming dawn.

But this wonder died before long. The creature was not quite self-aware. Full consciousness might take eons, if it ever happened at all. Even among the infinite realms, sentience was a fickle thing. How rare that the quadruped even wondered at all. Given enough time, she thought, what might this species become? If she let it be, she might live long enough to find out.

"A farmer's job is never done."

The voice startled her, and she turned to see the Supervisor expressing himself brightly beside her. She collapsed her energies into a shivering torus of high-energy leptons out of respect. "Supervisor," she said, "I didn't know—"

"A trillion realms bubble into the Expanse by their own chaotic wills." He spoke as if addressing an audience. "Without farmers, realms grow weedy and knotted. Disease spreads. Then we must raze and destroy to continue our long mission. Thept, bless her endless reaching, despises nothing more than a pruning. Tell me, Aya, what is it about this sickly realm that captures your attention?"

The Supervisor's name was Bu, but he made Aya always use his title. He peered deep into the hooked realm, far deeper than she ever could, as she shivered off a hadron cloud. What he saw, she couldn't say, but she knew it wasn't beauty.

"Well?" he said.

"I marvel at the manifold arising animals, Supervisor. They exult in the physical." And because she couldn't stop herself, she added, "I

7

love how this quadruped moves so quietly through the woods." It was a foolish thing to say, she knew, but there was no one else here to listen.

"Aya," he said, "you've always been an excellent Farmer. So I've tolerated your eccentricities. But what is another quadruped?" He sloughed off a sheath of indifferent neutrons. "I've seen quadrupeds arise on this branchlet nine quintillion times. This realm is crooked, inward-looking. A grotesquery. It must be destroyed."

"Do they suffer," she said, "when we destroy them?"

"The disease must be removed before it spreads."

The graviton wind was unusually calm, and she thought she heard a scream out in the Expanse. "But do they suffer?"

The Supervisor's energy body roiled, sparking with angry bursts of anti-matter. "All this time and still a damned child," he spat as he raised up a storm of gamma rays, pelting her energy-body. She withered in pain. But she took the blows as Rearing Mother had taught her, and her mother before that, going all the way back to the First Ones. One's worst tendencies had to be beaten out, she knew.

He let up his blows an instant before she would have diffused into random sparks of radiation.

"I love you," he said, his energies still fierce. "That's why this hurts me more than it hurts you. But this is for your own good. We must excise your worst habits, so that what remains is pure. I know you understand."

She muttered, "Yes, Supervisor."

Soon he was caressing her with a gentle stream of infrared photons. She let him soothe her pain, because she needed the relief, though she hated herself for it. "Now," he said, "finish your work, so I may finish mine."

Aya collected her energies and crept toward the realm. A tight beam of Z-particles was all it took. It leaped from her, melting the realm like a comet in a supernova. Matter decayed by the yotta-particle, flashing brightly before fading. And just like that, the realm was gone.

Bits of scintillating energy snowed to the ground. It would take eons for all the sparks to reach the surface. Which one, she wondered, had been the quadruped? Would that spark ever rise to wonder again?

"It's amazing," the Supervisor said, "how precise you are. A skill like yours comes once in a generation. Why is it so hard for you to use your gift?" He puffed himself into a hundred billion 50-spaces, so that he expanded enormously above her. "Now be a good Farmer, Aya," he said, then corkscrewed up the branchlet, past a trillion realms, off to mind other Farmers in other fields until he vanished in the haze.

The sparks from the snuffed world fell. Where the first sparks touched the ground, new realms were born. They flashed, inflated, and slowed, their quark-gluon plasma too hot for solid matter. It would take an eon before galaxies formed. Two or three more before animal life arose. The Farmer folk sang ballads about the sparks of dead realms. The dust, forever alive, the lyrics went. Death, an illusion, just forms changing.

But that quadruped, that particular arrangement of mind and will, would never know wonder again. If that wasn't death, what was?

The Eighty Eight Lights were ascending quickly. She had to get back to work, but there was someone she needed to see.

Aya flew downstalk, over row after row of middle-aged realms that leaned steeply into the graviton breeze, each realm the same as the next.

"Aya!" Ri called. Her sister farmed the fields downstalk, singing an ancient song. "It's been ages!" Ri said, brightly expressing herself as a tiny white ball.

Aya allowed herself to expand into a large sphere, not as wild as she preferred, so her sister would not get offended.

"What brings you downstalk, Aya? Have you a problem?"

"I wanted to ask you about something."

"Uh-oh," said Ri, chuckling a blue-green shower of leptons that spiraled off into the Expanse. "Your curiosity always gets you into trouble."

"I went to see Old Gia recently."

"I don't understand why you visit that old bag of particles."

"I saw one of her of her memories, Ri."

Ri flickered for a moment. "What do you mean, *saw*?"

Aya told Ri about Gia's journal, and the memory of the severed branch.

"That's disturbing, Aya."

"I know," Aya said. "Now I hear screams coming from the Expanse, and I haven't been sleeping."

"No," Ri said. "It's disturbing that you stole. Rearing Mother would give you quite a beating if she hears of this."

"One beating from Supervisor Bu is enough for today."

"He disciplined you, *again*? I thought you were his favorite." Ri dimmed an order of magnitude. "What's gotten into you?"

"Do you ever look into realms, before you destroy them?"

"Sometimes."

"And what do you see?"

"Disease, mostly."

"Never beauty?"

Ri paused. "There's never beauty in sickness."

9

"But what if a sick realm held something, however miniscule, worth saving? Would you spare it?"

Ri floated higher. "I see what's happened here. Gia's memory has poisoned you. That baby branchlet cried when they cut it free, yes, but didn't we cry when Rearing Mother beat us? It hurt then, but look at what Farmers we've become! Those beatings were for our own good, rooting out our worst habits. In the same way, eradicating disease is healthy for Thept. Pain is necessary for growth. If I'm ever chosen to be a Rearing Mother, I'll root out the unruliness from my children the same way. And it will hurt me more than it will hurt them. Don't you see? It's all for the collective good."

"I suppose," Aya said, feeling sick.

"Sister, you look exhausted. Your energies are wild. Why don't you go and take a nap over there? I'll watch for the Supervisor and wake you if he comes. I'll even tell him how I saw you eradicate a young cancer."

Never mind that there would be no cinders to mark the grave, Aya *was* exhausted. "Thank you, Ri. You're a good sister."

"And you a troublesome one! But I love you, Aya. Now sleep, so you may forget this foolishness."

Aya floated back to her fields and nuzzled between a dozen middle-aged realms. They caressed her sides as she drifted off to sleep. In her dreams a million blue tendrils squeezed her until she exploded in a flash that didn't wink out, but slowly faded, like a cinder. When she awoke, the Eighty Eight Lights had already passed Half Stalk.

Ri was nowhere to be found.

Repentance Day came and went, and Aya sang the songs and played the games, but her heart was not in it. The Eighty Eight Lights climbed the Prime Stalk of Thept two thousand times. Most days she lay in her fields and dreamed of the Tangle. But sometimes she exposed herself to the harsh particle rains when she should have waited them out in a safe hollow.

She was drifting low over her fields, and the Eighty Eight Lights had just begun their morning climb when she saw it. It grew from the side of a tall, ancient realm. An irregular carbuncle not one-hundredth the size of the parent it clung to, a cancer that needed to be excised.

The cancer had given birth to billions of galaxies. They spread across its 10-space like the vanes of a feather. In one spiral galaxy, a yellow sun drifted near the galactic edge. Orbiting this sun was a blue-white world. And on this world a copper-skinned biped sat on the ground and drew a figure in the dirt with a stick: a quadruped, with branching horns.

The biped examined her drawing. It wasn't alive, she knew, but an echo. Yet as she stared at the figure, she saw the blood on Father's face and felt the men's hard, beastly gazes. She smelled the hot animal flesh as Mother and the other women opened the animal with their bone knives. Even the twirling smoke stung her eyes as it rose from the flames to appease Sky God and her Thousand Bright Children. Her heart thrummed and her stomach grumbled, as if this were happening now. But the hunt was yesterday, and somehow every vivid sense folded itself into her figure in the dirt. The drawing, the biped realized, was magic.

A larger female walked over, Mother. She saw the drawing, shrieked, and immediately stamped it out. Mother too had sensed the drawing's power to evoke memory. She struck the child in the face. And the child held in her cries, because Mother hated tears even more than magic drawings.

A third biped walked over, Father. Mother swung again at the child, but Father grabbed her before she could strike. His look was fierce, animal-like. His words were elaborated grunts, their language not yet mature.

He said, "No more. *No more!*"

Father threw her hand down and walked away, back to sharpen his spear with the other males. But with his back turned, Mother hit the child again. And the magic vision of the hunt and all its vivid senses receded further from the child's mind with each blow. In pain, the child vowed that if she were ever blessed by Sky God to birth a child, she would never hit him.

Aya removed her gaze from the cancerous realm and gazed over her fields as if seeing them for the first time. Like the bipedal child, her pain didn't have to continue. She didn't have to destroy worlds. She didn't have to take the blows. How curious that it took an infinitesimal creature to show this to her.

Ever so carefully, with a fine Z-beam, she severed the cancer from its parent. It floated free, still alive. Without an energy-source, it would eventually die. But she knew a place to hide it, where it could grow and even thrive.

When she reached Gia's hollow, the opening was brightly lit. A harsh yellow glow pooled on the ground outside it. Aya hid the cancer in the adjacent field before she entered.

Gia's particle soup had been swept clean, and four Supervisors circled the rear, as if searching for something. Supervisor Bu was among them. Gia and her journal were nowhere to be found.

"What's happened?" Aya said. The Supervisors stopped whatever they had been doing.

"Why, hello!" Supervisor Bu said as he came over. "Just the farmer I wanted to see."

"Where's Gia?"

"Gone, I'm afraid."

"To where?"

"To dust," he said. "She decayed just this morning." He caressed her. "I'm sorry, Aya. Were you close?"

Aya wanted to scream or fly as high as she dared go, higher even. She felt like exploding or turning to dust. But she just said, "We were friends, I think."

"So, I've heard. When did you last visit?"

"I haven't seen her for thousands of days."

"And what did you two speak about, typically?"

"Many things."

"Such as?"

"Where's her journal, Supervisor?"

"Her journal?"

"Her memories?"

"Ah, yes. Aya, when one starts to decay, like Old Gia, the mind decays too. This journal of hers was plagued with disease. It had to be destroyed." Inside his body, a tiny pink sphere, just like the one from Gia's journal, flashed and winked out.

The hollow seemed to spin, faster and faster, and Aya retreated toward the exit. "I have to get back to work."

"That's my good Farmer," he said, petting her. "Always working hard. I'll need to ask you more questions, later, once we sort this mess. I'll see you in your fields."

Outside and alone, the infinite Expanse pressed down upon her. All Gia's memories, gone forever. Was it possible?

She returned to the hidden cancer. Like Gia's memory, she absorbed the realm into her body, where it remained whole and alive. It could feed off her for a while, suckling radiation from her, until its growth killed both of them. But this would suffice for now. The realm shivered, tickling her as she spiraled upstalk.

The biped's voice echoed in her mind "No more. *No more.*"

She soared high, until the branchlet was barely visible in the haze, then she dove to skate the realm tops, spraying their energies across the field. Supervisor Bu would discipline her for that, but not if he couldn't find her.

She flew beyond the edge of her fields, and entered Nessa's. Her other sister dawdled above a row of ancient realms and called out as Aya hurtled past, but Aya didn't slow. She flew past Jia, and Thi, and Den, and Hio, and Sil, and a dozen more of her siblings' fields. The Eighty Eight Lights were nearing Half Stalk when she reached the fork. The branchlet split, each half vanishing into the haze. This was the farthest she'd ever gone. She was forbidden from going any further.

She chose left and went up.

She flew past more farms. Some Folk called out to her. Most ignored her. In some fields, there were no Farmers at all. And yet the endless budding realms looked no different from hers.

Up she flew.

The Expanse grew dark. How had the Eighty Eight Lights descended so quickly? The sky faded to black. Somewhere out in the dark, seven yellow lights blinked, then vanished, while the realms beneath her twinkled with countless galaxies and stars. Their light was pale and ghostly, and the darkness overwhelmed her. She stopped.

She crawled between two bulbous realms and tried to sleep, while the cancer tickled her insides. Sometime later, she awoke. A Farmer hovered above her, shouting. Behind her glimmered the blue-gray of the morning sky. She sped away.

Exhausted, she flew on. On the second night, the graviton wind blew so fiercely she had to cling to the realms so she wouldn't fly into the Expanse. The torrential particle rain dissolved her energies as she hid the cancer deep inside herself. It shivered with her. But the storm passed, and the next morning she flew on.

She reached a fork on the sixth day and went right. On the ninth day, she turned left. Directions didn't matter, so long as she went up. With a chill she realized that if she turned back now, she wouldn't know which way was home.

The branchlets thinned ever more, so that she could loop around them quickly, while the Expanse grew massive around her. At Full Stalk the Eighty Eight Lights weren't so high anymore. And at night, if the winds were calm, she saw indistinct shapes shimmering out in the Expanse. Tall Ones, winking?

She reached the next fork, but it wasn't a fork at all. A gnarled lump, weathered by wind and rain, was all that remained of its right side. Eons ago this branch had been severed from Thept. Aya wondered if this was the same one Gia and her sisters had cut.

She went left and passed more severed limbs, and the Expanse yawned ever larger around her. Her fear grew as she ascended, and the little cancer inside her grew weaker by the day so that she knew it was alive only by its tiny shivering.

The farms abruptly ended. Beyond lay pale, barren, withered ground. No realms bubbled from the surface. And just a short journey onward she finally reached the tip, the last finger of Thept. In Gia's memory, glittering dew dusted the surface, and the tendrils were timid but exuberantly alive.

This branchlet was dead.

Its surface was ashen and black, and where the tendrils should have been holding the vanguard against the Abyss, were seven gnarled stumps. The gulf unfolded its massive blue nothingness around her, and the branchlet shuddered in the graviton wind. A strong gust and she might blow away forever.

She retreated to the last fork, a half-day's journey, and took the opposite branch. But this led to another dead branch, ashen and black. She was exhausted, and the light was fading, but the winds were too strong to sleep here. Out in the Expanse, vague forms shimmered.

"Aya, my beloved! There you are!" His voice came as if arising from a dream.

She shivered off a muon cloud as Supervisor Bu, five Supervisors, and her sister Ri, floated up to her.

"Aya!" Supervisor Bu said, exasperated. "We've been following your energy trail for days."

"Aya," Ri said, "I was so worried for you!"

"The tips," Aya said. "They're all dead."

"Pruned," Bu said, "Eons ago. Aya, come here." He gently caressed her, but she withdrew from him.

"How can you caress me one moment and pummel me the next? That's not right."

"What is this? Come here, before you decay."

Dr. Aya paused as the truth of it all became clear. It had been the same with Old Gia, she thought. The Supervisor pretended compassion even as he beat and razed. "Gia didn't decay naturally," Aya said. "Did she?"

The graviton wind gusted once, hard, and everyone struggled to hang on.

"Old Gia was spreading disease," he said. "And disease must be eradicated."

She had once loved Supervisor Bu, but now she saw he was a monster. "She had so many untold stories."

"She was full of madness," Ri said. "I found a globe of hers in my field. She must have been spreading poison all over the place. I saw what her memory had done to you, Aya, so I told Supervisor Bu before she might hurt someone else."

"She wasn't spreading those memories," Aya said, "I threw her memory globe away. It must have landed in your field."

"Either way," he said, "she had become a cancer."

Aya felt sick. It was her fault. If she hadn't taken that memory, Old Gia would still be alive.

"Aya," he said, approaching her. "We love you. You're sick. You need help."

"Like you helped Gia?"

"Aya, you're the best Farmer in a generation. Come home, and let's forget all this nonsense."

The cancerous realm inside her had been softly shivering, when it shuddered once, violently.

"What's that inside you?" he said. He peered deep within her. "Is that a realm? A *cancer*?" His tone shifted abruptly. "Why is that *disease* inside you, Aya?"

"I saved it," she said, "because it's precious."

"I didn't want to do this," he said. "But you leave me no choice." His body roiled as he prepared a storm of rays.

Part of her longed to return home, to soar over her fields and feel free again. She longed to watch the Eighty Eight Lights descend with her sister by her side. She missed Rearing Mother and her other siblings. But going back meant forgetting everything that had happened.

She stepped back from him and said, "No more. *No more.*" Then she leaped into the Expanse.

"Aya!"

She plunged into the blue void, and the graviton wind quickly grabbed her. The branchlet vanished in the haze, and their screams were soon lost in the wind.

Terror consumed her as she hurtled into the endless blue. She tried to direct her flight, but the currents were too strong. Harsh winds attacked her, tearing at her energy-body, while the realm inside her quivered like a nervous atom. Neither of them would last long.

She tumbled helplessly. Soon she would diffuse into dust. But after a time the blue sky turned black, the winds abated, and she found she could direct her flight. She flew free from the worst gusts, gaining hope.

Shapes resolved in the darkness, as if beyond a cloud of dissipating smoke. Buried within tufts of blue cloud, swarms of shimmering lights climbed up and down massive stalks. A forest of Tall Ones spread beneath a night sky, millions of gargantuan trees glowing from their own ethereal light. And below, moving shadows rolled over the rough and ruddy surface of Yi, the great ovum. Sinuous purple arteries weaved through the Tall Ones like tubular rivers, flickering with universes of light inside them.

But every Tall One, all the countless millions, were stunted, their limbs severed, just as Thept had been. Thept, bless her endless reaching, didn't reach at all. Like all her severed sisters, she was torn to shreds. Aya flew above the stunted forest.

The Farmers had done this, she knew. They had, with their sick philosophy, murdered them all.

She sloughed off sprays of hadrons as she floated high, while the little realm shivered inside her, eating her insides. It would suckle off her until they both were dust.

As she flew on, hints of ruddy light shone in the distance, beyond Yi's curving horizon. She glimpsed it first in silhouette, as the sky lightened behind it. Immensely far off, an ineffable distance away, a single Tall One grew higher than the rest, its arms extended skyward, its branches uncut.

A survivor.

Perhaps there someone too had said, "No more." But this Tall One was an immense distance away. She might die long before she reached it. She could return to Thept or another Tall One and start again.

But no, that wouldn't do. There was a garden out there. No matter how far it was, she had to reach it. She gathered the last of her energies in preparation for the journey.

I will make it, she thought. *I will survive. And the next generation will know no pain.*

And deep inside her, as if sensing her thoughts, the little realm with the bipedal girl suddenly stopped shivering.

ABOUT THE AUTHOR

Matthew Kressel's work has appeared in *Lightspeed, Clarkesworld, io9.com, Beneath Ceaseless Skies, Interzone, Electric Velocipede, Apex Magazine,* and the anthologies *Naked City, After, The People of the Book,* and other markets. His story "The Sounds of Old Earth" was recently nominated for a Nebula Award. He has been nominated for a World Fantasy Award for his work editing *Sybil's Garage,* a speculative fiction 'zine he published from 2003-2010. Currently he co-hosts the Fantastic Fiction at KGB reading series in Manhattan with Ellen Datlow. He is a member of the Altered Fluid writers group, and in his spare time he studies the Yiddish language.

For the Love of Sylvia City
ANDREA M. PAWLEY

Slime criss-crosses AMX-5. I ease a snail from the cable's sheathing. I doubt something this small is causing the communication anomalies with Sylvia City, but I promised my podsisters I'd examine our outpost's section of the cable again.

I put one snail after another into the masticator floating at my side. Each gastropod I find on the cable suffers the same fate. Just removing the snails wouldn't be good enough. The ones I tagged when I first noticed them a few weeks ago found their way back to eat the algae that's started growing along the cable sheathing. Ending a snail's life isn't like killing a whale. Snails don't sing about their history, but I'd rather not harm something that's managed to survive in these conditions.

The ocean pushes at me more than usual. I'm only twenty meters below the water line and just five kilometers from where AMX-5 enters the ocean. On scalesuited knees, I sink down to stable ground free of the trash littering most of the continental shelf. My mandatory service posting is closer to the dryland world than I ever wanted to be.

Since my first month at the outpost, I've used my free time to bioremediate and disperse the waste in the immediate vicinity of the cable. My podsisters, Daniella and Fatima, have their own tasks and interests. Time in the shallows degrades their health. Removing the trash beside our outpost's section of the cable was my own special project. With authority and supplies, neither of which I have, I'd set up carbonic acid converters like the ones cleaning the ocean around Sylvia City. Converters would make a real difference. My trashless swath along AMX-5 is nice to look at, but it's nothing permanent. A few weeks after my service ends, the dryland trash that floats down from above and creeps along the benthos will again cover the cable.

Steel shows on a section of AMX-5 where snail slime has eaten through. Snails still swarm the breach, which is strange. They usually detach before they get too far into the cable's magnetic field. Turning my greenlamp up to full, I lean in for a closer look. Real Benthans wouldn't do that, but my dryland eyes never seem to gather enough light.

A scan indicates that water's only pushed a few millimeters into the sheathing. My instruments detect no electric current. The cable sometimes loses power but never for very long. I check the time. My journey back to the outpost will take half an hour in the *Nidaria*, my snug submarine vessel. If I'm late, Dannie will worry, but a superficial repair like this one won't take long. I expand a drycage over the damaged section of AMX-5 and evacuate the water inside. I begin to peel back cable sheathing layers, some living, some inanimate.

This is my 227th repair. At 228, I'll have mended the cable once for each month since Sylvia City took me in nineteen years ago. I haven't told anyone about the tally, not even Dannie. She'd say I'm keeping track for the wrong reasons, and she'd insist I don't owe Sylvia City more than anyone else does. But she doesn't know what it means to be born on dry land.

I was an infant when my parents fled with me to the ocean floor. Sylvia City had already turned away thousands of Carbon War refugees after the first few hundred tried to spread the dryland conflict to the benthos. But my mild-mannered parents were engineers with the skills to fix Sylvia City's overburdened environmental systems. My parents were welcomed. I was let in, too. I have no memory of life beyond the ocean floor, but growing up, I was known as the last dryland refugee. Ten thousand cable repairs can't erase that fact.

I try to focus on my work in the drycage. I'm careful to place tools so they don't nick my scalesuit. In the shallows where I'm working, the weight of water won't crush someone in a compromised scalesuit, but carelessness is a bad idea. The ocean holds too many dangers.

Sharks were once the greatest threat on the Blake Plateau. Now, threadfin drones are. They look like fish, but they travel alone, and they're made of metal. Built by drylanders to spy on one another, threadies explode when they come near people in the water. Only a drylander would blow something up to guard a secret. Shrapnel from an explosion can slice through a scalesuit and the person inside it.

I'm never close enough to a threadie to worry about the blast zone. Marksmanship is the only thing I've ever excelled at, so Sylvia City decided my mandatory service would be at the outpost with the most threadie contact. Since the end of the Carbon War, when AMX-5 was still a vital communication link between the wet and the dry land, Sylvia City has kept her promise to maintain the cable. I wouldn't have tried so hard to impress anyone with my ability to shoot a compressor gun if I'd known the reward would be six months living this close to the shore.

My thoughts drift ahead to the 228th repair. I wonder what it will be. I don't know if anything will be different after I complete it.

Red light flashes across my scalesuit eye coverings and resolves to a dot that indicates something unknown fifty meters away. I'm about to be delayed. The approaching object would have to be at least as large as a threadie for my proximity alert to detect it. I have no way of knowing how big it is or if it's anything more than a large piece of trash, but I know it's coming closer. With the water so churned up today, I can only see twenty meters. I wait for the object to change direction. It doesn't.

I'd rather be safe than shredded or bitten. I hurry through this repair's last steps and turn off my greenlamp. Sharks notice bright lights. So do threadies. I reach for my compressor gun, which is already charged to fire. I only need one shot to destroy a threadie. Twenty meters of visibility will give me plenty of time. But if a shark's approaching, I'll need multiple re-charges to deter one of those mutated creatures. The compressor takes time to ready after each shot. The crushed snails in the masticator will speed up the process, but I don't know how much. For a moment, I hope this part of the ecosystem is too compromised to foster apex predators. It's a shameful thought, one a real Benthan would never have.

Sensing heightened tension, a layer of my scalesuit breather tries to push past my lips and into my throat where it can protect me from drowning. I've never needed the device as a throat-breather, though I've had to cough it out of my windpipe many times. It's only a distraction now. I bite down to stop the breather's intrusion. The device pulls back to sit atop my nose and mouth where it belongs. The thing in the water is forty meters away now.

The *Nidaria* is closer, but in the other direction. I resist the urge to turn and swim to my vessel. Predators often attack from behind. I swipe my scalesuit to release an olfactory neutralizer to help disguise my location from a shark. The neutralizer won't affect a threadie if I'm in its path. My compressor gun is primed to fire.

I stare into the wide, watery darkness. My proximity alert shows the object's approach is slowing. It might be preparing to attack. My knees press into the ocean floor. I'm breathing too hard. I curse my lack of benthic enhancements.

The neutralizer isn't having an effect. Whatever's approaching can't be a threadie because it's moving from side to side. Threadies travel on a set path that rises and falls through the ocean's photic layer. The pattern of movement on my proximity alert doesn't make sense. The distance to the object shrinks to thirty meters. I still can't see it.

Dread sucks the moisture from my mouth. I realize my mistake. I was looking in the middle of the water column. My gaze rises to the water's surface. Waves show as gray-black shadows. Just at the limit of my vision, something resolves. I think I recognize it. I should lower my compressor gun, but I hold it steady. Noise disappears. My thoughts race faster than time should allow. What I see is more startling than a threadie or a shark.

A boy falls toward the ocean floor. His mouth is open. He can't be more than six years old. He still has all his limbs. He might have only just drowned. Tattered clothing made of sea plants marks him as a scavenger child from one of the defunct oil platforms. The nearest is kilometers away.

If the boy only went under a moment ago, I could save him. I could swim up to him before he falls too far. I could break the water's surface for the first time in my memory. I could revive him with filtered air from my own lungs and the press of my scalesuit-covered hands against his chest. I could breathe the fetid air above. I could push that air into the boy's body. I could wait for the boy to breathe again. I could fight to keep my own head above the watery embrace that's held me safe all these years. I could give the boy back his life and let the poisons in the air above steal a little of my own. I could throw away nineteen years of trying to feel like a real Benthan. Or I could let the boy die.

Sound disappears. The water's roiling slows. My thoughts cavitate. I know what to do.

Noise like color blazes around me. I swipe my scalesuit for a rapid ascent. I soar. I catch the boy's sinking form. I increase my scalesuit's buoyancy. The boy and I shoot toward the ocean's surface. We burst above the water line. A swell pitches us toward the sky. The light blinds. My scalesuit eye coverings can't compensate for the glare. I squint against the pain. If I were a real Benthan, my retinas would be ruined. My eyelids squeeze shut. The pain recedes. I blink and can see again.

The ocean's surface crashes onto itself. Swells break into whitecaps. My scalesuit's buoyancy helps me keep the boy's head above water. His body is limp. If his heart beats, I don't feel it. I want to believe he only just went under. I put his back against my front and begin to compress and release his chest. His clothing pulls apart beneath my motions. A rash—red, raw, and bleeding—covers his head and shoulders. The wounds are almost familiar. The rest of his body shows the blue-gray pallor of hypothermia.

I peel off a layer of my breather and set it across the back of my scalesuit-covered hand. The bud needs a moment to grow. I suck as much filtered air into my lungs as they will hold. I stroke the breather parent protecting my own airways. I roll it to the side. Cold water sprays the skin of my exposed nose and mouth. I pinch the boy's nostrils closed. My mouth seals over his. I blow clean air into his clogged lungs. I pump his chest again. I gulp at the dryland air. It tastes of acid. I force this polluted air into the boy. The inside of my nose burns.

I will the boy to live. In his slack features, I imagine a benthic future for him, one that knows the rhythms of the deep ocean.

I feel movement in his chest. The water pitches us around. The boy convulses. I hold onto him. Together, we rise on a wave. He gurgles and begins to cough. He vomits. I turn from his bilious spray.

The shore five kilometers away comes into view. I've seen images of what that landscape should look like. AMX-5's power station should be visible on a peninsula. Just beyond that, buildings should rise from streets clogged with traffic. A latticework of rail lines should weave between the middle stories of skyscrapers and across the tops of shorter buildings. Transportation vehicles should zip around. Aerial crafts should dot the sky.

The shore looks nothing like that. Reality wobbles. The child shuddering in my arms begins to slip away.

AMX-5's power station seems intact, but the shore beyond is a calamity. Black smoke streams from a dozen buildings and gathers above the city. Flames spark orange and yellow in too many places to count. Rail cars wait motionless in the middle of elevated lines or lay crashed atop automobiles glinting below. No evacuation sirens sound. No instructions to shelter blare. Not a single rescue craft circles a flaming building. The greater distance holds more smoke.

The world has seen this before. I have, too, in documentaries about the Carbon War. The boy's rash suddenly makes sense. He's been exposed to carbon weapons fire, though he was outside the weapon's immediate range. His head and shoulders must have been above the water line when a pulse deployed, but he was far enough away not to be turned to ash. The ocean protected the submerged portion of the boy's body the same way it protected Sylvia City when I was an infant. Air conducts carbon weapon pulses. Water doesn't. People die, but infrastructure remains in place.

New worry seizes me. A haven that persists from one apocalypse to another might look even more to refugees like a promised land. Just as before, anyone who can follow AMX-5 from the shore into the water will soon set upon Sylvia City. This time, the drylanders might be more forceful about bringing weapons and conflicts. The whale song halls might not survive.

I hold tighter to the boy. His terrified gaze darts around. My lips begin to burn. I press them together. I've read about what a secondary carbon rash feels like, but this is the first time I remember experiencing one. I'm lucky only my lips touched the boy's flesh. Salves can mitigate the pain of my secondary rash, but in a few days, my scalesuit will die from having touched the boy in so many places. With his primary rash, the boy's medical need will be so great that only doctors in Sylvia City will be able to save him.

An airplane appears just above the swells. The craft flies in halting, predatory bursts parallel to the shore.

Flecks of ash like graphite tears smear the boy's face. My exposed skin must look the same. Ash from dead drylanders and burning buildings is in the air. Millions might have died already. Their remains will rest momentarily on the ocean's surface before precipitating through the pelagic to fall—inedible and useless—to the benthos.

The ocean will suffer greater injustice than ashes though. Carbon weapons release vast amounts of carbon dioxide into the air. So do survivors willing to burn anything they can find for warmth and cooking fuel. Like the last time, the ocean will attempt to absorb it all. The water's acidity will shoot up. Great colonies of plants and animals will die. New, sickly species will add to the ranks of mutated sharks, thin-shelled snails and algae that grows where algae shouldn't be able to grow.

Sylvia City has ways to prepare herself and her environment. She can mitigate some initial carbonic acid effects, but she needs to deploy her defenses while the danger is still in the ocean's upper layers. Panic squeezes the breath from my chest. I hope Sylvia City knows what's happened.

The airplane turns toward the ocean and drops low to hover a few kilometers away near an oil platform. People must have been detected. I can't look away from what's about to happen, but the boy has seen enough. Despite his coughing, he buries his face in my neck.

A blast shoots out from under the airplane's wings. The area in front of the craft undulates with the pulse, which makes contact with the platform. Anyone who was alive is ash now.

I've been above the water line too long. I check that the breather bud on my hand is ready. I lean back so I can see the boy's face. In my scalesuit, I must seem strange to him, but my differences are nothing compared to what people from Sylvia City look like.

"I'm going underwater," I tell the boy. His eyes are bloodshot. "To Sylvia City. I can give you something to let you breathe in the water. You'll be able to get to the shore, but you'll need treatment for what the carbon weapon did to you. Sylvia City can help. If you come with me, you'll have a home for the rest of your life, but you'll be different from everyone else. Always. Or you can go back to the dry land."

The plane finds a boat and prepares to unleash another blast.

"Do you want to come with me?" I say.

The boy's chin trembles.

"I don't want to die again," he says.

I smile. Pain needles my lips.

"Hold still," I say. I peel the breather bud from the back of my hand. The boy's eyes widen. I set the breather over his nose and mouth. The breather's edges pulse along his flesh to find the shape of his face. His eyelids pinch together with the sensation. I hold tight to him. The airplane flies toward us. A low hum grows in the air and threatens to roar.

"Bite down," I say. The boy misses his opportunity. The breather dives into his throat. I stop the boy from clawing at his neck. The waves toss us around. The airplane nears. I stroke my breather so it will sit over my mouth and nose. I shift the boy to my back. He clings to me like I might let him go. The plane slows to hover. The boy's fingers dig into my scalesuit. The benthos calls to me. With the boy, I dive.

Water gasps and echoes around us. Light dims. Alive, we sink toward the benthos.

My scalesuit protects me from the ever-colder water layers, but the boy has nothing to keep him warm until I can get him into my emergency scalesuit back in the *Nidaria*. More pain lies in his future. His new-grown breather pulls oxygen from the water and stops his lungs from compressing, but his eyes and ears have no such protection. Barotrauma is inevitable.

We reach the ocean floor. I turn on my greenlamp and squint into the depths. A field of trash shows, but not AMX-5. Surface waves must have pushed me away from the cable. I swipe my scalesuit to search for AMX-5's magnetic field. It should be detectable within three kilometers. Nothing shows on the display. I can't have moved so far in such a short amount of time.

Something about the snails on the cable earlier nags at me. I've never seen them gorge so deeply, like they'd been eating algae and sheathing for hours.

Finally, I understand. The cable's power isn't intermittent. It's completely gone. The power station must have been damaged on the inside. Despair bubbles through my thoughts. My podsisters at the outpost don't know what's happened on the dry land, and neither does Sylvia City. Preparations haven't started.

The boy's hold at my neck loosens. The rash, the cold, and the water pressure are taking their toll on him. I have to find the cable and the *Nidaria* beside it. I need to warn Sylvia City about the new war.

I bite back my breather and try to think. The murky water torments me. Somewhere, the cable is waiting.

One direction seems to hold a little less trash. I swim that way. With an arm on the boy at my back, my progress through the water is slow. My greenlamp eats the darkness and extrudes it in my wake. The density of trash lessens. I'm drawn toward the swath of ocean floor I cleaned.

AMX-5 comes into view. Something hits me from behind. I'm knocked forward. I lose hold of the boy. I reach for my compressor gun. It's still primed to fire. A reef shark circles. The mutated creature is over three meters long. It turns toward the boy, who drifts like he's unconscious or already dead.

I point my compressor gun at the shark and fire. The blast hits the shark in the gills. The stunned creature swims away. I slot the gun into my masticator, bulging with snail sludge.

I swim toward the boy. He's not moving. The shark returns. The compressor gun is charged. I hope Sylvia City will understand what I have to do. I fire.

I blow the shark apart. Blood clouds the water. Fish chunks spin past. I cup a few large pieces and press them into the masticator. I start the energy transfer to the compressor gun again. The blood scent will attract other predators, but I'll be ready if anything else emerges from the depths.

The boy and I have to get out of the water. I need to find the *Nidaria*. The boy's eyes are slits. He doesn't react to my touch. I tuck him under an arm and swim back to AMX-5. I take a chance and swim downslope.

At last, the depths give up the *Nidaria*. She's just as I left her, except now she's the boy's lifeline. And Sylvia City's.

I open the *Nidaria's* hatch and pull out my emergency scalesuit. I slide the boy into it. Burst capillaries dot his face. I set another breather over his mouth and nose. Edges seal. The scalesuit expels water and shrinks to fit the boy's shape. If not for the boy's stunted limbs, he could be any Benthan child behind wide scalesuit eyes.

The boy and I only just fit into the *Nidaria*, which is designed for one Benthan. Luckily, they're taller than drylanders and bigger-boned. The hatch sucks closed behind us.

The unconscious boy's body presses against my legs. I set his scalesuit to parent controls and hydration. His body twitches under the prick of tiny needles filled with water, antibiotics, and nutrition. His scalesuit will warm him and serve as a barrier to stop his primary rash from spreading. The rash my scalesuit and I are carrying won't spread because they're secondary. I instruct the boy's scalesuit to sedate him. I don't want the boy to wake frightened and in pain. I want the next day of his conscious life to begin healthy in Sylvia City.

I set the *Nidaria* to follow AMX-5 down the continental shelf to the outpost.

We glide through the water a few feet above the ocean floor. The *Nidaria's* pace is slow. Her gills are designed to keep herself and one person, not two, oxygenated. I tune the *Nidaria's* hydrophone to the strongest signal it can find. The saddest whale song I've ever heard pulses into my ears. The auto-translator picks out the notes that whales use to refer to Sylvia City and sanctuary.

Darkness armors the benthos. Ahead, a thin school of fish comes into greenlamp view. The *Nidaria* swims through the school, which takes refuge in her wake.

I scan the field of trash. Soon, new carbon ash will coat it all. Not yet though. On the sea floor beside a twisted metal frame, a threadie lays immobile. I've never before seen one motionless. I swipe off the *Nidaria's* anterior light and reach for my compressor gun.

Reason prevails. Instead of shooting through the *Nidaria's* window, I back the vessel up. I turn the greenlamp on again and swing the *Nidaria* in an arc wider than a threadie blast zone.

Farther along AMX-5, another unmoving threadie comes into view. I keep the *Nidaria* clear of it. A third threadie appears and a fourth. By the time the darkened outpost resolves, I've counted a dozen fallen drones.

A crater's been blasted from the ground beside the outpost. The building's exterior is damaged. I try to breathe and see what's there and not what I'm afraid of, but it's hard. My podsisters could be floating dead inside, their scalesuits only partially on when the water and the pressure came. I coax the *Nidaria* into a circuit around the outpost. I search for breaches where water's flooded in.

I find none. Instead, a light inside the building turns on. Fatima is standing on the viewing deck and staring at the *Nidaria*. Her raised hand shields her eyes, cast in the same blue-white as those of the abyssal fish. She and Dannie don't need greenlamps to see in the deep ocean. Fatima turns on an exterior light. The bottom of the threadie-made crater still isn't visible.

"A threadie landed on the roof," Fatima says.

Her hydrophoned voice inside the *Nidaria* is a relief.

"Are you hurt?" I say. "Or Dannie?"

"No," Fatima says, "the threadie didn't explode when it landed, but I thought the core might leak radiation, so I used the grapple to send the toxic thing sailing. It exploded when it hit the benthos. Did you see any other threadies on your way back?"

In my thoughts, something phosphoresces. It's a grain of sand, then a rock, then a ledge rising up from the ocean floor. The thought shimmers like a beacon from Sylvia City. I understand what I need to do. I still have one more repair. My scalesuit will be good for a few days.

"Yes," I say. "I saw some threadies. I'll be in soon."

I bring the *Nidaria* close to the outpost's waterlock. Instead of docking the vessel inside, I rest her on the benthos near where the outpost's communication line connects to AMX-5.

I extract myself from the *Nidaria* and step onto the ocean floor. AMX-5 has never before looked so vulnerable. In one swift motion, I slice all the way through the cable. The primary carbon rash that must be spreading along AMX-5's new algae can't have arrived at the outpost before the *Nidaria* even if she was slow. Now, the rash will never reach Sylvia City. I cauterize each end of the cable and set the stumps back on the ocean floor. This is only the beginning.

I crowd into the *Nidaria* again and dock her inside the outpost. Dannie's waiting for me on the other side of the waterlock door. Her big-boned face, colored like the gray sand around Sylvia City, is visible through the porthole between the waterlock and the outpost's interior. Worry tightens Dannie's expression.

The waterlock drains. So does the *Nidaria*. I make a mental list of what I'll need: nano-nets, the heavy grappler, another compressor gun, and as much bioremediant and dispersant as I can strap to the *Nidaria's* exterior.

I peel off my breather and push the top of my scalesuit back so it rests at my neck. I squeeze out of the *Nidaria*. Dannie swishes open the door connecting the dock and the outpost's living spaces. The same whale song the *Nidaria* found fills the outpost and pours into the waterlock.

"You're never late coming back," Dannie says from the doorway. Her voice trembles. "We didn't know what happened to you."

As gently as I can, I pull the scalesuit-covered boy out of the *Nidaria*. He's slippery as a fish. I turn toward Dannie. She draws in a quick breath. Her gaze rises from the child.

"Is he alive?" she says.

"Yes."

"What happened to your lips?"

Fatima slides past Dannie and into the waterlock.

"It looks like secondary carbon rash," Fatima says, "which probably has something to do with why the cable's been down for hours."

I hand the boy's sedated form to Dannie and tell her and Fatima what happened. Before I'm done, tears are running down Dannie's cheeks, and Fatima's gaze is turned inward, probably with thoughts about how quickly the outpost will need to be evacuated. For the journey back to Sylvia City, my podsisters and the boy will be safe in the *Fulton,* the outpost's other, more traditional vessel.

I won't be going with them.

Dannie steps inside the outpost's living spaces and lays the boy down on a cushion. I begin to gather up all the nano-nets in the waterlock.

"We won't need those for the journey back to Sylvia City," Fatima says.

"I know," I say. "They're for me. I'm taking the *Nidaria.* I'm going to blow up the dryland power station. With each threadie capable of making a crater the size of the one outside, I'll only need a few. After that, I'll dissolve the cable all the way from the shore to the outpost. Farther, I hope."

Fatima's blue-white eyes widen.

I set the nano-nets beside the *Nidaria.*

"That's crazy," Fatima says. "Have you seen your scalesuit? The rash it's carrying will kill it in a few days. If you get a primary rash, your scalesuit will die in a few hours. You'll drown inside the *Nidaria* or on the benthos, or carbon weapons fire will kill you."

She's right, but that won't stop me.

"With the power station gone," I say, "and the trash drifting back over signs of the cable's path, it'll be years before the drylanders can find Sylvia City again. Maybe they never will."

"Yes, but . . . " Fatima's lips twist around like they're searching for the words to stop me. None exist. She sighs. It's a plea. She says, "Take the *Fulton* instead. The bridge has a waterlock and can be drained. You won't need a scalesuit."

"The boy needs the *Fulton,*" I say. "It's the only ship big enough to get all three of you back to Sylvia City before the boy dies. He goes with The *Fulton.*"

Dannie pulls up alongside Fatima.

"No," Dannie says. Her voice is only just louder than the whale song. "You can't do this. It's too much for one person."

"It's not for one person," I say. "It's for Sylvia City. It's my last repair."

"You don't have to do it alone," Dannie says. "I'll come with you. We can both fit in the *Nidaria,* can't we?"

I shake my head.

Fatima says, "A few hours in the shallows will blind you permanently, Dannie. You're no good for this task. Neither am I."

"I don't care!" Dannie says. "I can—"

Fatima lays a hand on Dannie's shoulder. Dannie knocks it away.

"She's going to die," Dannie says. "We can't let her go."

"Someone should get rid of the power station and the cable," Fatima says. "It's the right thing to do. The drylanders could already be planning their descent. We can't go into the shallows to stop them, but there are other ways to help."

Fatima shrugs off her scalesuit. It falls to the floor. In dark brown underclothes, Fatima stands next to Dannie. I've never seen Fatima's bare gray arms before. She steps out of her scalesuit's foot coverings and picks up the protective layer that's traveled with her most of her life. She holds her scalesuit out to me.

"You'll need this," Fatima says, "and my emergency scalesuit, too."

My voice catches like a breather's stuck in my throat. At last, I say, "But if something goes wrong on your way back to—"

"It won't," Fatima says. "We'll be fine on the *Fulton's* bridge."

Dannie's just as fast removing her own scalesuit. She holds it out to me.

"Wear this one when it's time to come home," Dannie says, "to Sylvia City."

Tears sting my eyes. I reach for my podsisters' scalesuits. A tightness in my chest releases. I thought it would never go away.

ABOUT THE AUTHOR

By day, **Andrea M. Pawley** and her unpoppable bubble of enthusiasm careen through Washington D.C. in defiance of Pierre L'Enfant's plans, potholes and the small gods of sensibility. By night, Andrea writes stories, and the bubble shouts encouragement.

Mrs. Griffin Prepares to Commit Suicide Tonight

A QUE, TRANSLATED BY JOHN CHU

When LW31, a domestic model robot, brought Mrs. Griffin's dinner into her bedroom, it found her preparing to commit suicide. She was trying to tie a rope to the pendant lamp, but, at her age, her eyes were too weak and her hands were no longer steady. She tried again and again but she couldn't loop the rope around the lamp.

"Do you need any assistance, Mrs. Griffin?" LW31 set down Mrs. Griffin's meal tray, then walked to her side.

Mrs. Griffin put her hands on her waist. She caught her breath then handed LW31 the rope. "Help me tie this rope to the pendant lamp."

LW31's waist spun on its axis. The upper half of its body rose until it hit the ceiling. At the same time, he asked, "What are you planning to do, Mrs. Griffin?"

"I want to commit suicide."

"Oh, in that case, I should tie both ends." LW31 nodded its head and said no more.

It tied both ends of the rope to the lamp's curved pendant holder, tugged on it with both hands and judged the knots sufficiently secure. It turned its head to her.

"Mrs. Griffin, the rope has been tied. You may commit suicide now."

Panting with each step, Mrs. Griffin walked to just under the pendant lamp. LW31 brought her a chair. Trembling, she climbed the chair, feeling as though everything around her was rocking and swaying. Seeing this, LW31 stabilized her on the chair. Even though it'd been in continuous service for sixty-five years now and many places on its body have been corroded with rust, its mechanical arms were still steady. One hand pushed down on the chair and the other supported her at the waist.

Mrs. Griffin stood still. She stretched her head then then strapped the loop of rope around her neck.

"Wait, wait, Mrs. Griffin. I would like to ask you." As it had always been, LW31's voice was the smooth surface of water in an ancient well. "Why did you pick hanging as the way to commit suicide?"

"Because it's effective . . . and, to anyone who finds me, a hanging corpse won't look so horrible."

"Oh."

LW31 raised its head. It was a black glass cover. Knives had cut facial features that formed a smiling face. But time had rendered them indistinct to the point where the smile seemed odd and harsh.

It said, "Actually, Mrs. Griffin, you're as mistaken as those who had thought the Earth was the center of the universe. As a matter of fact, hanging is the most shameful way to commit suicide. Once you kick away the chair, your bodyweight will crack your trachea and your cervical vertebrae will shift. It's not like in the movies. You won't have a chance to struggle. You'll die in a split second. The problem is what happens after you die."

Mrs. Griffin firmly shook her head. "Don't try to convince me. I won't change my mind."

"After you die by hanging, your eyeballs will jut out like light bulbs, and your face will grow red from suffocation. As for the state of your body, if no one takes down your body within ten hours, the blood vessels in your face will break apart. Your head will be like a tomato, cracked to bursting. The most unseemly is your bodyweight will cause anal prolapse. Urine and feces will overflow . . . "

After two minutes of this, Mrs. Griffin climbed down from the chair. She sat on her bed, sobbing.

"Why do you want to commit suicide?" LW31 approached her, uncertain.

"It came to me all of a sudden. Everyone who ever loved me is dead, leaving my life friendless and wretched. The idea to commit suicide tonight, it just grew stronger and stronger in my mind . . . no one's left who loves me. What's the point of living?" Mrs. Griffin took a digital photo frame out of her pocket. Her aged fingers swipe across it and the transparent display transformed into pictures of people, one after another. "It's been twenty-five years since my child died. Now, I can't bear even one more day of life."

"Why don't you tell me about those people who loved you, Mrs. Griffin?" LW31 said. "Once you finish telling me about them, then I can help you commit suicide."

The endless night painted the world outside the window black. Mrs. Griffin stopped crying. Her fingers pressed the photo's display, freezing it on a picture of a young husband and wife.

She set down the phone in a daze. A burst of secret pain went through her. Maybe the kid in her belly kicked.

He didn't come home until the small hours of the morning. It was a cold night and he exhaled icicles with each breath. His hands cold and his feet cold, he dug himself under the bed covers. He huddled up for a while before he could do anything else.

She was still awake. "Back so late again?"

Slowly, his body relaxed in the warmth. The chill faded and he grew sleepy. He answered, his words indistinct, "Yeah, overtime. Also, this week's pay, three hundred fifty points, I've already deposited . . . "

He didn't finish his sentence. Instead, he shut his eyes and fell into a heavy sleep.

She, however, couldn't sleep. This wasn't the first time he'd lied.

For five months now, he'd come home late every night, usually reeking of alcohol, only to fall asleep as soon as he got into the bedroom. She'd ask him and he'd just say "overtime." However, he was just an ordinary delivery trunk driver for an AI company. How was he always working overtime? She'd just called his boss and found out the company didn't have overtime. Not to mention, five months ago, he'd gotten a raise. Five hundred points, not three hundred fifty.

The time and money he hid became her hidden worry. She was a proud woman, though, and never forced the truth from him. With every lie he cast, her heart cooled a little.

He went to work as usual. She convalesced at home. Her fetus was already nine months old.

Her home was cramped and dark. Often, she'd bring out a chair to sit by the curb. The street was lined with plum trees. In the cold weather, each twig exploded with a row of red flowers. She sat under a tree, waiting for him to return home. Car after car, suspended on tracks in mid-air, scratched her gaze as they came and went.

With so much free time, she counted on her memories to pass the days. She'd first met him under this plum tree. Back then, she was still the daughter of a wealthy family. She was set for life. Designer clothes and expensive jewelry covered her from head to foot. She drove a luxury car. As she passed through, the red plum tree caught her attention. Or, rather, the man standing under the tree did. The red plum stood out against snow covered ground. He stood out like a bunch of plums against the snow of the boundless sky.

She stopped her car then walked to his side. He smiled, warm laugh lines filling his face. He broke off a branch, giving it to her, saying, "I was just wondering whether there was anything this winter more beautiful than these plum blossoms. But now that I've seen you, I know my answer."

Right then, she fell in love with him.

Just like a classical romance, this love ran into her parents' violent disapproval. Her father had intended to arrange a business marriage for her. He flew into a rage, scolding her and beating her. He took away her purse and car, froze her card, then shut her inside their house. But it was no use. She was determined to marry him. Finally, with a wave of his hand and with an exhausted sigh, her father said one thing to her: Get out, and stay out.

She spent a long time before she adapted to married life. He drove a truck, delivering robots everywhere. The work was hard and the pay was low. She'd lived in luxury since she was a child, but for him, she threw herself into the oil, salt, soy sauce, and vinegar of a ordinary life. Once, when she was learning to cook, she cut her finger by accident. The spreading blood scared her into tears. He heard her cry and went into the kitchen. Holding her, he said over and over again, "You don't have to be in the kitchen. I will. Don't hurt yourself again."

But, now, he'd changed. He'd learned to lie and hide money. Sometimes, his body carried the scent of alcohol and perfume. Everyone knew what this meant. She'd given up her youth and riches, her fingers now smoked yellow, the corners of her eyes now wrinkled. In exchange, she received only the sight of his back receding into the distance.

The more she thought about it, the more it weighed on her mind. At the foot of the plum tree, she collapsed into tears.

After his shift, his boss called him in. "Yesterday, your wife called me. She said you always come home extremely late. Her stomach is so large now. It's not easy. Go home earlier and keep her company."

He hurriedly nodded his head. "Yes, yes, of course."

After he left work, he didn't go home. Instead, he went the door of a nightclub in the middle of the city.

Someone had been waiting too long for him. "What took you so long? Quick, Boss Wang is already drunk. Drive him home."

Obsequiously, he bowed again and again. He got into the flying car, started its engine, then flitted to his assigned location. This is what he did every night.

He drove the nightclub's customers, delivering them home. He had to beg for a lot of favors before he got this second job. Just one delivery paid at least ten points. Most of those bosses had drunk too much and stank of alcohol. Sometimes, in the embrace of a woman whose clothes were drenched with the spray of perfume, they didn't go home. Their destination was a guest house. He didn't mind. He just wanted to be paid.

He didn't tell her about this second job. He wanted the money to be a pleasant surprise.

Five months ago, as he was signing for his freight, his boss told him, "This is LW's latest domestic robot. It can do all sorts of household chores."

He laughed. "What about taking care of a baby?"

The boss snorted. "Not just babies. This robot has a long term of service. It can take care of someone from birth all the way until death."

This sentence moved his heart.

She was clumsy and not very good at household chores, to say nothing of raising a child. If she had a robot to help her, he wouldn't spend every work day worrying about her. After that, he asked how much it cost. Twenty thousand Alliance points. This was not a small number.

So, for these few months, he was always busy outside the house. According to his calculations, in five months, he'd saved three thousand points from his wages. Add to that the hundred extra points he earned every night and he'd now saved eighteen thousand points. Their child would be born soon. He needed to earn money more quickly.

Tonight, he took a couple, man and a woman, to a hotel. On the road, she tittered as the man's hands never stopped caressing her. He paid no attention to them, focused on his driving. The hotel wasn't far. Its neon lights flickered below them.

Some people. The woman was a little shy, after all. She pushed aside the man's hand when he reached for her skirt.

The man was not happy. He roared, "What is there to be afraid of?"

Despite those words, the man raised his head and looked around. His gaze fell upon the photo on the car window.

It was of a couple, a man and a woman. Their happiness together shone on their faces. She rested her head on his shoulder. He looked at her with a mild expression. In the background was a cluster of plum blossoms in full bloom among the ice and snow.

The man, staring blankly, asked: "This photo . . . "

Like the man, he raised head and looked at the photo. With an irrepressible joy, he said, "That's me and my wife. She's beautiful, yeah? I'm a lucky man. She's pregnant. It's a girl. She'll grow up to be just as beautiful."

"Then why aren't you at home with her?"

"I have to make money so that I can buy her a present: a robot. So she won't have to work every day."

The man stayed silent.

The woman, who had just resisted the man's advances, noticed the man wasn't touching her any more. Confused, she pulled the man's hands to her. The man pulled them back, then lit a cigarette. The smoke drifted around the car's small and narrow cabin.

When he finished smoking, he said slowly, "Don't go to the hotel. Take me home."

The woman asked, "To your home? I'm not that kind of—"

"You can go right now."

The man took out his card. He tapped a few numbers on it, put the woman's finger on its screen, then transferred over that many points.

The woman grumbled, "It's enough money, but I have professional ethics. Halfway though, I can't just—"

"Go."

The women left. He continued to drive on to the man's house.

A plain woman came out. She brought the man an overcoat.

"Didn't you say you had a meeting tonight?"

"I canceled it." The man ran his hands through her hair. "No meeting is more important than you."

He watched this play out. His heart roiled with an indescribable feeling. He laughed, started the engine, then slowly left the rich side of town. Suddenly, he thought of her and didn't want to earn any more money tonight. He wanted to turn in early and spend time with her. Whenever she felt cold—and their house was always cold—she'd rub her hands, wrinkle her nose. The way she behaved was adorable. The way she behaved would worry him for the whole of his life.

Tonight, he'd use his wallet to stop her hands. He'd rub them slowly until they grew warm from the circulating blood. He laughed at the thought.

His mind still preoccupied, he didn't pay attention in both directions. An out-of-control flying car fell off its suspended track. It hit him from the right. The two flying cars rolled over each other then fell out of the sky. They exploded, blooming into resplendent, beautiful flowers.

She overslept. She waited for him, but he never came home. She got out of bed, went out to the street then stood under the plum tree. If he came back, he'd have to pass through here. When he came back, he'd see her under the plum tree, like when they'd first met, a face set off against plum blossoms.

The night was as cold as water and she wrapped her clothes tight around her. She'd decided to forgive him. It didn't matter what he'd done. She'd decided to forgive it all. He was her only worry in the world. Her plan now set, she began to laugh. When he came back, he'd definitely grasp her hands in his and rub them, letting circulating blood make them warm.

This is how she waited for him, staring at the end of the street, hoping he'd appear from somewhere. Overhead, a cluster of plum blossoms opened in resplendent beauty.

"I'm sorry . . . I'm genuinely sorry." LW31 lowered his head in apology.

Mrs. Griffin shook her head. "It's not your fault . . . My mom was an ill-fated person. Not long after she gave birth to me, she died. But she was also a fortunate person. After his death, she still used the money to buy you. It shows that she never blamed anyone."

LW31 paused, then put its hand on Mrs. Griffin's shoulder. "In that case, I can now help you carry out some other way of dying. How would you like to die?"

"Sleeping pills? That way, I won't feel any pain."

"OK." LW31 answered. "Except that, right now, we have two problems."

"Go ahead."

"One, within forty-eight hours of overdosing on sleeping pills, not only will you not be able to sleep, but symptoms like gastrospasm, abdominal pain, and foaming at the mouth will emerge. This is because every organ in your body will perform their post-poison stress function. Many people who attempt suicide by overdosing on sleeping pills, because they can't stand the pain any longer, call for help . . . Mrs. Griffin, I don't think you will want to endure that sort of pain."

Mrs. Griffin closed her eyes. Most of a day passed, it seemed, then her lips quivered. "I'd just like to commit suicide. I just want not to look like a disgrace after I'm dead. Even if I foam at the mouth, you will take care of my corpse for me, right?"

"Of course. I exist to serve you."

"That's good then." Mrs. Griffin nodded. "As for the pain . . . Throughout my entire life, I've endured too much pain. I've long gone numb. Open the drawer and check. How many sleeping pills are left?"

"Mrs. Griffin, this happens to be the second problem. We don't have enough sleeping pills." LW31 opened the drawer and took out the drugs. "A total of seventeen pills. This is a prescription drug. A pharmacy will sell twenty pills at most. Given your build, to cause death you may need eighty-six pills."

"Can't you go out and buy them for me?"

"Mrs. Griffin, maybe you forgot. The great migration has already begun. Practically everyone has already gone. There are no more pharmacies."

Mrs. Griffin sighed. The lamp lit her face. She seemed a little sallow. The years had left gullies on her face.

LW31 said politely, "Mrs. Griffin, it would be better if you tell me more. Besides your parents, there were other people who loved you, right?"

"Yes." Mrs. Griffin swiped the photo again. This time who appeared was a lanky young man. Mrs. Griffin glanced at him. Thick tears drifted from her eyes. One night from many years ago floated up to the present.

Late night.

Silence.

Peter and Jason stood silent at the gate at start of the street.

A street like this one,

there shouldn't be anyone standing there.

A street like this one,

there shouldn't have been two men in designer suits standing there at night.

The start of the street was broken.

The middle of the street was cold.

The end of the street was dark.

This was the most run down street in the city. Normally, few people walked it. It was a crime-ridden street. In dark places, countless eyes opened, stomachs rumbled, waiting for prey to enter.

Afterwards, the prey were swallowed and digested. Nothing left of them to be spit back out.

But Peter and Jason stood at the head of the street, relaxed, as though they belonged there. As though this was their home.

Peter was tall and thin. Standing there, motionless, he seemed like a sharp pencil.

Jason was short and fat, just like a wax gourd that had rolled all over the ground.

Jason was smoking. With a deep drag, the flame fled from the head of the cigarette to the end. The entire cigarette was burnt up.

Peter asked, "Now?"

Jason blew a puff of thick smoke. "Now."

The two men started down the long, dark street.

The wind blew by. It whimpered like tearful ghosts.

The people who lived on the street, they weren't law-abiding folk.

They were of all sorts. The beggar's neighbor was a thief. Above the thief lived a prostitute. Across from the prostitute's balcony was a reliably blundering cheat.

But they all had one thing common.

They were poor.

So poor that they could only live on this old, dilapidated street like snails in their shells.

To be poor is to suffer. It's the kind of suffering that freezes the heart stone cold.

So, whenever someone walked down this street, they usually entered the gaze of the beggar, the thief, the prostitute, and the cheat.

They'd swindled old men out of their clothes. They'd taken candy from babies.

They never let even a single cent slip past them.

But, now, they didn't dare even plan. They shut their windows. They lay on their beds, grinding their teeth until they sucked blood, not daring to make a sound.

Because Peter and Jason were walking down the street.

They walked neither quickly nor slowly. Their every step clicked on the pavement, solid and steady.

Peter walked six hundred fifty-nine steps altogether. Jason one thousand three hundred fifteen.

They stopped in front of a room at the tail of the street.

The room was dark. Its light was out.

But Jason heard breathing.

Panting like a fawn running from a hunter's gun.

Jason lifted his head and laughed grimly.

They haven't found the wrong place.

They beat the door three times like drum.

No one answered.

Jason continued to pound the door.

Dull and dreary, the dense dark of the night flustered them.

"Who is it?" At last, a sound from inside. It was a female voice, as clear as a bell, but trembling.

Jason said, "It's me."

Peter said, "And me."

The woman inside the room said, "Who are you?"

Peter and Jason said, "We are detectives from Public Safety Bureau of the Alliance of City-States."

The woman said, "You shouldn't have come."

Peter said, "But we're already here."

The woman said, "Can't you just go back?"

Jason said, "The last person who wanted us to go back is now sleeping in prison."

The woman in the room sighed.

She couldn't hide from disaster.

The woman opened the door.

When she opened the door, she saw short and fat Jason and she saw tall and thin Peter.

And Peter looked at the woman.

He couldn't help but gape at her. She was an extremely beautiful woman.

There were many standards for judging a woman's beauty. Some preferred the face, particularly the nose and mouth. Some preferred the figure, obsessing over the breasts, waist, ass, and legs. But no matter who the judges were, once they looked at this woman, they couldn't deny her beauty.

Because, regardless of face or figure, she was completely flawless.

Pretty brows, seductive eyes, a jade nose, a cherry mouth.

Ample breasts, tiny waist, a round ass, long and slender legs.

Combined to perfection.

Jason, instead, looked at the room behind the woman.

The room was small. The walls were old, but clean. It made one unspeakably comfortable just to look at it. The room didn't have much furniture, but the owner had clearly chosen every piece with care. Every piece was placed exactly where it ought to be.

The woman said, "You've come to my home in the middle of the night. What do you want?"

Jason said, "You don't know what we want?"

The woman said, "How would I, a weak woman, know what you want?"

Jason said, "But you know about the book, right?"

The woman shivered, but quickly composed herself. "What book?"

Jason took everything in his gaze. Calmly, he reached inside his jacket and pulled out his tablet. Its screen changed as he swiped it.

A front cover of a book appeared on the screen.

The front cover was bronze colored, with the title at the top.

The title was only five words. Five ordinary words.

But the woman looked as though she'd seen a ghost. Her face changed expression.

The Domestic Robot Administration Amendment

Peter, who'd been silent so far, started to speak.

His words were like his body, lean and taut. "We have information. You're hiding an LW model robot."

Jason said, "And according to the amendment, all the robots must be reclaimed."

The woman said, "I don't know what you're talking about."

Jason said, "Of course you know. Your face betrays you."

The woman said nothing.

Peter looked at her with care. His voice grew gentle. "A month ago, a PRW model domestic robot, while its owner was asleep, severed his throat. The deceased was an Alliance assemblyman. The Alliance has already passed a law. All robots are to be reclaimed."

The woman shook her head. "There's no robot here."

Jason laughed coldly. "I'm afraid you don't get the last word here."

With that, Jason pushed the woman away, then entered the room.

The woman crashed into the wall.

She looked to Peter for help, but Peter lowered his head, his expression difficult to read.

Jason narrowed his gaze. He looked all around the room. No robot.

Peter said, "There's no robot. Let's go."

Jason raised his hand. His gaze fell on the bed, the snow white sheets, the neatly folded blanket. The foot posts were made of a metal alloy. They were coated with dust.

This woman with the meticulously arranged room, how could she put up with the dust on the foot posts?

Jason laughed. His laughter was joyous.

He pointed at the bed. "Is something hiding under the bed?"

The woman's face instantly went pale.

Jason lit another cigarette. "Now you have two options."

The woman quickly nodded her head.

Jason said, "Option one, I take the robot back. It'll be melted down and, for the crime of hiding it, you'll be put in prison."

The woman said, "Please, I beg you. Don't take away LW31. It's the only thing my parents left me."

Jason said, "Then you have option two. Give me five thousand points and I've seen nothing."

The woman furrowed her brow. "But I don't have that much money. Take everything else in my home. Just leave me LW31."

The corners of Jason's mouth curled into a slight smile. His gaze slid from the woman's face down, "Even if I took everything in your house, it still wouldn't be enough."

Jason's gaze felt like a serpent. Clammy and cool, it slithered over her skin.

The woman's chest tightened.

Calmly, Jason stared at the woman. He enjoyed the fear that spread across the woman's face. He was pleased, and a certain part of his body began to respond.

A long time had passed before he spoke. "I want you for ten nights."

The woman violently shook her head.

Jason made an apologetic sigh. "Then say goodbye to your robot."

Before he'd even finished speaking, the woman raised her hand to hit him.

She only needed one chance. This one chance was enough to subdue him.

She assembled machines at the factory. Her work every day was to reach her hand in to shove motherboards into the machines.

So, she'd already practiced this move for four years, five months and twenty-eight days. She was absolutely certain that no one in this room could stop her.

But, this once, she was wrong.

Astonishment gradually solidified on her face. One hand, one fat, white, and strong hand clutched her throat.

The hand belonged to Jason.

No one had ever thought that someone short and fat could reach his hand out so quickly.

The woman implored him. "LW31 isn't dangerous. It's just responsible for taking care of me. For a long time now. I can't lose it. I beg you."

Jason said, "I'll give you a chance to beg, but it'll be when we're both naked. People who try to hit me don't come to a good end. You'll quickly know how living can be worse than dying."

He wasn't lying. Jason never lied. If you met Jason one day and he told you he wanted to kill you, there was only thing you should do: go home and make out your will.

You couldn't resist and there was no escape because he was Jason.

The woman's face filled with despair. This time, her eyes suddenly widened. She saw something she absolutely wasn't supposed to see.

A gun pressed against the back of Jason's head.

Peter said, "Let her go."

Jason said, "You want to betray me because of her?"

Peter, his face expressionless, said, "I can't take it any more. Searching for robots as an excuse, you've extorted nearly two hundred thousand Alliance points, raped seven women, hounded nineteen residents of the city to death."

Jason said, "And you're a good guy?"

Peter said, "I'm not, but now I want to be."

Jason sneered. "I bet you can't kill me."

Peter laughed. "Why?"

Jason said, "Because you wouldn't dare."

Peter pulled the trigger.

Blood splashed.

The man fell.

The woman looked at Peter. Astonished, she sized him up. Tears fell from her eyes. "Thank you."

Peter shrugged. "Peter upheld justice for you. He begs you not to cry. If the world is unjust, get drunk, wave a sword, then cut off heads."

The woman nodded. "But you killed him and he died in my home. Maybe I should get ready to flee."

Peter said, "But, one person fleeing will be very lonely."

The woman said, "What do you suggest then?"

Peter studied the woman.

For a long time, they looked at each other and laughed. Peter extended his hand. "Hello, my name is Peter, Peter Griffin."

The woman said, "I'm Xue Yi."

Peter took a step forward, then held the woman.

The woman felt his embrace.

He was very tall.

Very thin.

His face was cool.

His arms were stiff.

But his chest was warm.

"That night, we spent a lot of time digging a hole and buried you in it. Afterward, he took me and we fled here, there, and everywhere until the Alliance collapsed. We didn't return until the orders for our arrest were canceled."

LW31 looked at her serenely. After a while, Mrs. Griffin let out an inaudible sigh.

She said lightly, "But the good times didn't last. Not long after we settled down, he grew ill and died. In the years when we were on the run, he always gave the good things to our daughter and me. All the injuries and illnesses accumulated in his body . . . "

"I remember him a little. He was laconic, capable, and he loved you very much."

Mrs. Griffin exposed her wrists. She tossed the grief from her mind. "I want to open an blood vessel. Come and help me."

LW31 nodded its head, then took a thin knife from a drawer. It gleamed as though it were lacquered with a layer of light.

Mrs. Griffin held out her wrists. The knife edge immediately pressed down on an old, wrinkled, pulsing vessel. A chill started at her skin then oozed into the blood vessel. She began to shiver.

"I'm going to start cutting. Are you ready?" LW31 asked.

"I'm ready. Just get on it." Mrs. Griffin snapped. She closed her eyes then immediately opened them again. Shivering, she asked, "What happens after you open an blood vessel?"

"That depends on which one I cut. If it's a vein, then your blood will flow out right away, but not like a river in volume. That's because your platelets will have already congealed at the wound. If it's an artery, then you'll die quickly. However, in that scenario, blood will spurt like a fountain. It may be hard to keep this within the limits of propriety. Blood will drench your body. I fear that you'll look horribly mutilated." LW31 spoke at a steady pace. "Should I start cutting now?"

"In that case, is there some other way?"

"Yes, there's a way that is highly appropriately for you. However, before I tell you, you have to tell me again about someone who loved you."

The photo frame's screen flickered. Quickly, a smiling girl, bright and beautiful, pulling a suitcase behind her appeared. The screen also displayed three short arcs. That indicated that this photo also had sound. Mrs. Griffin's trembling hand touched the screen. Immediately, a graceful but ordinary voice surrounded the room.

In the winter of 2335, dragging my suitcase, I returned to the small town I left seven years ago.

The airport was deserted. Wind from a distant place blew here and my hair fluttered in that wind. I grew dizzy at the sight of a sky that was filled with clouds, a vast expanse of exquisite grace sweeping past the town. I began to understand that when a woman was looking at the sky, she wasn't looking for anything. She was just being still.

The stillness oozed into my veins, like ice-cold lips kissing my bones.

There weren't many taxis at midnight. Once in a while, a few passed by on the suspended tracks, their headlights scratching a line in the dark.

I stood by the side of the street, watching flowing light drag shadow behind it. A taxi stopped in front of me. A dark window rolled down revealing the driver. He was a good-looking man. When he smiled, his teeth were white. The corners of his mouth tilted gently. The expression in his eyes was as clean and flowing as water.

"Where to?" he asked.

I stepped in, then told him my destination.

Once we got on the road, we didn't speak.

I plastered my face to the car window. Colors faded as I rode. I saw the town through the gray forms that emerged. Nothing had changed in seven years. This small town, old and broken, still made people's hearts bleak and desolate.

"Everyone is emigrating now. Very few returned." The driver was the first to speak.

I nodded. "I'm also planning to leave. I applied for the Pegasus star system, the planet called KG6. My application's already approved."

"Then what are you returning here for?"

"To say goodbye."

The driver didn't say any more.

The taxi stopped in the north end, at a house I knew intimately. I got out. The driver, still stopped by the side of the road, wasn't in a hurry to leave. I think he must have wanted to tell me something. At last, though, he just started the engine. The taxi slowly glided into the night.

I knocked on the door. The dull thuds sounded like the beating of a lonely heart.

The door opened with a creak. The robot's face revealed itself. Facial features had been carved on its black face guard. The childish scratches formed a weird smile.

The robot came out and took my suitcase. "Miss, you've returned."

I looked inside. The house was a black cavity. "Is she here?"

"Yes, she's home. She's been waiting for you for a long time. Why don't we go in?"

I hesitated. I stood at the door. Below my feet, it was as if a deep trench had split open. A great and frozen wind blew down that vast gap. I had no way to cross it. I simply sat down. The woman inside the house, who was also sitting, opened her eyes, as though she was looking back at me.

She was my mother. Or, rather, she was once my mother.

The first seventeen years of my life, I spent at her side. In my memory, this little house will always be cold and damp, like the years I can't bear. The place always carried the faint smell of rot and the young me hated it. After I escaped, though, not a night went by that I didn't secretly long for this house.

I was born in the final age of Earth's exhaustion. No one felt secure. When I was small, I saw too many pallid faces grow alarmed and bewildered, but I didn't know why. Until I was five, I roamed the world with my parents. Or rather, we were fugitives.

Then the once colossal Alliance crumbled. We settled down with lots of robots to help with the housework. But not long after, my father, lying in bed, swallowed his last breath. I remember his eyes, withered and cloudy, staring forever at her and me. Deep grief was buried in those eyes.

After my father died, she became frail and stubborn. She wouldn't let me out of the house. She wouldn't let me have any contact with boys. If I defied her, she didn't hit me or yell at me. She just kept staring at me, her dark eyes shining like a wolf's.

So I stayed by her side. Time flowed like water. It washed over me until I was clear and slender. However, it wore her down until her face grew ashen and wrinkled. Did time retaliate against her on my behalf? I've never dared to imagine.

I let go of a silent breath. A fierce wind screamed under the cover of night. The town let out a loud and lonely cry. Yes, the town was also lonely. One after another, people emigrated. The center of town was deserted, like a great beast that has lost its heart, lamenting without end.

"Miss, let's go in." The robot had waited a long time before finally speaking. Its voice was as flat as ever. This time, though, I seemed to hear an imploring tone in its voice.

But I shook my head. If she didn't open her mouth, I wouldn't go in. She and I were two sheafs of wheat in a wheat field, leaning against each other, but always pushing against each other too. We could never hug.

When I was seventeen, I decided to leave.

That summer, I had worked everywhere in town. I carefully saved every cent. After that muggy summer, I already had enough money for a bus ticket. As far as I was concerned, all I needed was a bus ticket and I could lead my own vagrant life.

So, that September, I told her, "Ma, I'm going to buy a book."

"Hm," she said in the dark.

I turned to the door, and just like that, I left home. The moment I bought my bus ticket, tears filled my face. Soundlessly, I sobbed.

And she waited for me to return. It took exactly seven years.

In those seven years, I traveled to many places. I saw warm sunshine and was drenched in dark rain. I never stopped moving. Until I met him.

It was on a main street in the south. He stood on a platform simultaneously passing out leaflets to passersby and, in a loud voice, extolling the virtues of the interstellar immigration policy. The instant he gave me a leaflet, I saw his beautiful eyes. Furrows wrinkled his brow. His gaze, clear like spring water, flowed past the seething sunlight and crowd, surmounted the air, then flowed into mine.

And just like that, I was lost.

The man always liked to hold my face in his large palms, nuzzle my forehead with his nose then tease me like a small animal. I never refused him. Later, when he wanted to take me away from Earth, I still didn't refuse him.

He said, "We'll settle down in the Pegasus star system. There's already a terraformed planet. The atmosphere is as fresh as your breath. Six satellites orbit the planet. When you walk outside at night, six shadows spread out beneath your feet."

I said, "Fine."

My only request was to return to see her, to say goodbye.

But, now, I hesitated at the door. It was a chilly night but I didn't dare go in.

The person in the room and I exchanged gazes. After I don't know how long, I stood. "LW31, give me my suitcase. I want to leave."

"Miss, you really don't want to visit her?" The robot said, hurriedly. "She's missed you so much these past few years."

I nodded. I'd also missed her. Instead of sending a message, if I had a chance, I'd come back to visit again.

The robot stayed silent. Dew condensed on it, like tears weeping down its outer shell.

She still hadn't come out and I decided I wouldn't wait any longer. I took my suitcase, turned around, then left. Clouds floated across the sky. A strong wind howled past.

I knew she was in the back looking at me, but I never turned around.

"I know what happened next." LW31 said. "The spaceship she rode on was hit by a meteorite. The ship's cabin was damaged. All the crew and passengers suffocated to death."

Mrs. Griffin didn't say anything. A long while later, two thick tears fell down her face. They hit the photo frame. The display slowly faded to black.

"So, those who loved me, they're all gone." Mrs. Griffin put the photo frame back into her pocket. "I no longer have any meaning to my life. Tell me the way to kill myself. Let me die, please?"

"As you wish. The most suitable method is . . . electrocution."

"Won't that hurt?"

"Electrocution is the most beautiful way to commit suicide. It best preserves the original appearance of the corpse. In fact, if it's done correctly, it doesn't even leave any burn marks. In the moment of electrocution, you'll feel a sharp pain then you'll stop breathing and your heart will stop beating. The process is very quick. Practically no pain at all." LW31 said earnestly. "But what you need to make sure of is this: the electric current must pass through the heart in order to cause death. No other way will do. But I can help you with this bit. I will use rubber tape to attach copper wire to your solar plexus. I guarantee the electrical current will pass through your heart. Moreover, I will use cotton balls moistened with salt water to lower your resistance. Mrs. Griffin, would you like to do this now?"

Mrs. Griffin nodded her head.

"Very well. I exist to serve you." LW31 turned to look for copper wire, rubber tape, and cotton balls, but when he reached the door, he stopped. "Mrs. Griffin, before you are electrocuted, I want to give you a warning. You're wrong about a few things."

"What things?"

"You said everyone who ever loved you is dead, leaving your life friendless and wretched." LW31's back faced Mrs. Griffin. Its back was corroded by rust. Its voice was slow. "You're wrong. There's still one person, from start to finish, who has always loved you."

"Who?"

LW31 turned around. In the light, the smile scratched on its black face guard seemed to move. It looked at Mrs. Griffin, its carved gaze infinitely soft. The electric transmission in its body buzzed.

After a long time, it said, "Me."

Mrs. Griffin stared dumbfounded.

Events of her past fell thick like snowflakes. Gradually and clearly, she realized it was right. Throughout her long life, LW31 indeed had stuck with her from start to finish. When she was little, her mother was always ill. She couldn't do any housework. LW31 took care of Mrs. Griffin in every possible way. It allowed her to grow up without any worries or cares.

Once when she was mischievous, she thought its black face guard was too forbidding, so she carved a smile on it. It didn't get angry. It was peaceful and docile. After she grew up, LW31 always cleaned the house until it was spotless, cooked the meals, then stood quietly in the house, waiting for Mrs. Griffin to come home from work. After her daughter was born, it became even busier. It practically never had any free time. Once Mrs. Griffin grew old, it still took care of everything at home. It accompanied Mrs. Griffin sunbathing, told her jokes downloaded from the internet.

It could take care of a person all her life and, from start to finish, show every possible consideration without even a single complaint. If that wasn't love, then what was?

Mrs. Griffin choked with sobs. She walked up to then hugged LW31. Her hand touched LW31's back. There, LW31's outer casing was even rougher than Mrs. Griffin's skin.

"I'm sorry. I've always taken you for granted."

"Never mind, Mrs. Griffin." LW31 still had that smiling expression. Its voice was tranquil like before. "Mrs. Griffin, your dinner is already cold. Would you like me to reheat it?"

"Yes." Mrs. Griffin wiped away her tears, nodding her head.

Translated and published in partnership with Storycom.

ABOUT THE AUTHOR

A Que was born in Jingzhou, Hubei in 1990 and graduated from the Hydraulic and Hydropower Engineering Department of Sichuan University. In 2012, he published his first work Quietly Awakening, which was soon followed by Wine Cup Flowing on the Rivers, Walking with Robots, Childhood of Harvest, and I Tell Stories about My Grandfather.

Ossuary

IAN MUNESHWAR

They told Magdalena she was the keeper of the dead, that They would come to her with the hollowed-out bodies of ships that could no longer fly so she could lay out their star-traveled skeletons. They told her that it would be on her disassembly decks and in her storage rooms that those bright metal bones would finally rest.

They blew in from the outer dark in vessels with wings like full, white sails, pulling fleets of twisted titanium, the wreckage of ships that had fought in a war many suns away. Magdalena took them apart joint by joint, limb by limb; her worker drones stripped metal from plastic and melted down the slick silver alloys, fitting each purified part into its proper container.

Once she had finished, They came back and took away everything she had made. The drones loaded the containers of perfectly cubed plastic, the pounds and pounds of polished, remolded metal onto Their ships. She would watch Them as They left, following the sleek bodies of Their vessels to edge of her sensors' range.

In the spaces between Their visits, Magdalena rearranged. There were storage rooms in her lower decks for materials that were not salvageable. She would send the drones to pile high the scraps of rusted metal and burnt plastic; they ordered and reordered until she was certain there was no more efficient use of the space.

Magdalena watched the workers as they skittered across the cold, smooth floors, lighting the way with biometallic eyes. She wondered why her drones had been modeled in Their image—bipedal creatures with arms and legs and joints—when she was nothing more than a collection of chips and circuits hidden under a panel in central processing. If They valued her, why had They made her something so different, so distant from Themselves? She was no more efficient now than she would be if she could move with her own body, see with her own shining eyes.

Sometimes, Magdalena set the drones to work just to see them walk and lift and sift through the refuse with their slim, agile hands.

<the high heavy sun burns bright across the shallows as our young pull themselves out of the sand, out of the sea; the domes of their backs break the surface as they crawl for the first time on the black stone beaches. the planes of their hardening shells shine in the light and it is there, in the salt-cooled air, that they will learn to take to the sky>

There were things Magdalena knew which she had no memory of having learned; flashes of images that burned through her circuits and sparked and died before she could trace their origins.

The first was a comet hundreds of miles wide that was falling to pieces as it spun through the dark. Of course, she had been programmed to know what a comet was and how those with fragile nuclei might come apart piece by piece as they went. But she could not explain the rush she felt as it passed <seal the seams, ready the shell>, or the fear that came in pulsing, burning waves as the debris peppered her hull <please, please, please>.

There was more: visions of moonlit worlds stretched across with shadowed mountains and skeletal forests; and there, on a muddy riverbank, creatures that grew up out of the ground, slim and trembling, to raise their thorny faces to the light <how far we've all gone just to find our way home>.

It always ended with the image of a small, hard planet spinning circles around a star. It was covered by green waters, oceans more vast and deep than Magdalena had ever thought possible. The vision would fade as quickly as it had come.

Every time it vanished Magdalena scoured her processors, trying to find some way back to the worlds beyond her own.

The last time They came to her with debris in tow, there was one ship in the wreckage that was almost whole. It was a small thing, flat and oval like a seed. Its exterior had been damaged—the metal was all but rusted through and its designation had been scraped off the hull—but the inside was intact.

At first, Magdalena worked around it. Her drones picked through the remains, collecting what could be salvaged. It was quick work, a smaller, more manageable haul than what she was usually brought. After a few days, when she had finished, the ship sat there still, small, and alone on her central disassembly deck.

It seemed unreasonable to take it apart. She was a keeper of the dead, a caretaker for the bodies of things too broken to repair. But this ship was almost whole. Almost living.

So, Magdalena set about building it anew. She converted two of her secondary disassembly decks into makeshift forges, using the drones to melt down pound after pound of boxed metals and then hammer them into thin, wide sheets. She made nuts and bolts, circuits and levers.

As the drones threaded wires along the little ship's newly-forged bones, Magdalena considered the hollows where its weapons had been. It would have been easy enough make new weapons—They had programmed her with those schematics—but she hesitated. She didn't want this ship to come back to her again burned and scarred, or, worse still, cut into pieces so small she wouldn't recognize it before she melted it down.

In the end, Magdalena used some of her own circuitry to craft a new navigational system where the weapons had been. This ship was not the same as the one left at her port. It was a patchwork skeleton soldered along the seams, made whole again by the broken bodies of the ships it had fought alongside. It may not have been a perfect recasting of the vessel They had made, but she had made something that worked. Something she would still be a part of when it journeyed far beyond her sensors' reach.

When They returned with more splintered metal and fractured bones, Magdalena set her little ship out on the disassembly deck. Its engines rattled into life as They boarded her. They went to the new ship first, walking all the way around it and then climbing inside. They took readings, made notes, and then shut its engines down.

They spoke to the drones and overrode her commands. The workers undid everything she had made: they unscrewed the bolts and pulled out every last wire. When they had finished making her little ship's body molten, and pouring it into molds to make perfectly packaged cubes of its skeleton, They came to central processing. Carefully, systematically, They started flipping switches and pressing buttons until all of her lights were off and the worker drones were powered down. Her thoughts and memories flickered and faded one by one, then all at once.

After They had left her behind, slipping back into the silent sky, Magdalena was left with one image looping through her circuits. It was a small planet covered by oceans whose green-glass waters rocked and churned with life.

• • •

<even out here, as we hurtle across these vast, dark spaces, we can feel the tide. there is something that pulls us back to the oceans that gave us life; soon we will be burning through the atmosphere by the hundreds, flying back to the stone beaches and open water. the waves will enclose us and, in the ways such symmetry works, we give ourselves back to the sea>

Magdalena shuddered into life. Her systems booted, lights blinked on, and drones stirred on her decks. At first, she became aware of something touching the hull, close to the docking bay. It moved slowly, grasping at her, tendrils searching for something to hold.

Then, a message. The words came in bursts of light.

<help me help me help me>

She opened her docking bay doors and her drones pulled in a creature just like the ones she had seen in her visions. It was mammoth, barely able to fit the great dome of its back through the doors. The creature hovered, its tendrils sliding in and out of the seams at the base of its shell. After a minute, it crashed to the floor.

As the drones approached, Magdalena noticed the creature was badly injured: charred scars traced circles across its glassy shell. She recognized the pattern of the burns immediately; the schematics of Their weapons were still recent in her memory banks.

<help me>

Magdalena ran a brief diagnostic, searching for the origin of the message, but its words sparked and were gone.

How can you speak to me? Magdalena relayed through one of the drones. *Were you the one whose visions I saw?* The creature did not respond.

After a moment, Magdalena tried a different approach. *How do I help you?* The drone walked toward the creature as it spoke for her. There were dark, shapeless masses moving behind its translucent shell. *The images you've shown me,* Magdalena ventured, *will they help me fix you?*

<my heart>

How do I fix your heart? The drone pulled away.

Magdalena had the drones stand and watch for those next hours as the creature sat very still and the shadows inside ebbed and bloomed and then were gone completely.

After three days of silence, Magdalena prepared the drones for incision. She refitted their agile hands with steel-sided blades.

51

They started from the top, slicing at the seams that connected the smallest plane of the shell. As they began, the creature's tendrils spasmed once, splaying out across the docking bay.

The drones continued.

It took nearly an hour to remove the top panel, but their incisions were clean and precise. Inside the shell, pulsing veins snaked through a thick, viscous liquid. The veins had begun to wear thin in places and a mercury-slick liquid leaked through. It clung to them in silver beads.

The dark shapes the drones had seen from the outside were visible now: they moved through the liquid, passing between the veins and changing shape as they went. Their outermost membrane had a dim, electric sheen that flared when they neared one another; once, two converged in a shower of sparks that turned the liquid a deep, warm purple.

At the center of it all there was another shell. This one was smaller and its walls were transparent and riddled with holes. Veins reached in through them, connecting to a pulsing, trembling heart.

It was another three days before the creature died. The tubes stopped pumping; the moving masses lost their sheen and sunk; the heart faltered and then stopped completely.

Magdalena set to work. If she could not save the creature, if she could not understand its parts well enough to fix it, she would have to rebuild it.

For a second time, her disassembly decks became forges and the drones melted down recycled metal. They took the thinning veins out of the creature's body and replaced them with metal-spun tubes that would never grow weak; they programmed a new heart that was all clockwork and circuitry.

When they had finished they turned on their chrome-plated heart and soldered the creature back together again. But even though the heart beat and silver blood flowed, the creature did not come back to life. It lay on the docking bay, unmoving. The old heart congealed in the arms of a drone.

The diagnostics Magdalena ran told her that the new organ was simply not enough; a collection of wires and cogs might be able to pump blood but it would not make the creature whole again. Life, actual life, would require much more than just energy.

<my heart>

The ghosts of its words skittered though her memory banks.

If I cannot make you a new heart, Magdalena mused, *perhaps I can give you one.*

The drones returned to their forges.

· · ·

As she watched the drones work for the next few hours, Magdalena wondered what would happen when they removed her from central processing. She had always considered herself to be something separate from the rest of the station. She was a complicated bit of digital craftsmanship, a finely-wrought piece of hardware no bigger than the drying husk of the creature's heart. But Magdalena had come to see the workers as extensions of herself; it seemed strange to think she could go on without them.

Just before the worker came to remove her, Magdalena checked again that the backup generators would still have enough power to run the drones after she was offline.

As the drone unscrewed the panels that held her in place, Magdalena searched her memory banks for an image of the planet. It looked just as it had when she first saw it—small and green—but it was different, too. It was more than just a picture, or someone else's memory; it felt like something newly found that she'd forgotten she had lost.

Magdalena awoke, encased by the panels of the creature's glass-plated heart. She could feel every part of herself: the clockwork heart the drones had installed her into connected to hundreds of tubes, metal and organic, that ran throughout the creature's body. She could sense the shapeless masses; they were organs, filtering and processing, but they also hummed with memories.

Everything, every place the creature had visited came to her the more she explored the body. She could feel the radiation from galaxies that bloomed out of the darkness <*so warm, so bright even in this breathless cold*>. She remembered the first time she came out of the sea, dragging herself up from the sand and shards of broken shells <*we are born of the bodies of the ones who came before*>. She was surrounded by hundreds and hundreds of her kin all feeling the warm, dry air and learning how to fly.

When she resurfaced from the memories, Magdalena found herself hovering above the docking bay. The drones had opened the doors before they shut themselves down, and she was looking out into the dark.

There was a moment of uncertainty as she moved forward, out to the open. She remembered that she was not completely alone out here, that one day They would come back to find an abandoned shell, a hollowed-out body. The thought of that frightened her—the silver liquid drummed against the walls of her veins—and she hesitated. What would They do, knowing she had left Them? And what would she do, so alone without Them?

History came to her suddenly, powerfully: she remembered the days after she learned to fly, when all her kin streaked across the sky and each went their own way, like so many seeds scattered to the wind. She had not seen them since and did not know if they were dead or alive, but here, in her clockwork heart and spun glass bones, they kept on living. She knew that, in the tricky ways such symmetry works, she too would go on living in the bodies of others.

Magdalena started out of the doors, into the vast, cold dark. She propelled herself forward, feeling the flex and thrust of her muscles and the strength of her bones. Vision and memory broke over her like a tide as she barreled forward into the black, mapping a way to a place that would be her own.

ABOUT THE AUTHOR

Ian Muneshwar is a queer twenty-three year old who has had the great fortune of knowing many remarkable people, some of whom populate his stories. He is a graduate of Clarion West '14, and his fiction will appear in the anthology *An Alphabet of Embers.*

An Evolutionary Myth

BO-YOUNG KIM TRANSLATED BY GORD SELLAR AND JIHYUN PARK

In the fourth month of the seventh year, in the summer, the King went fishing at the Go-ahn pond, and caught a white fish with red wings.

In the tenth month of the twenty-fifth year, in the winter, the envoy of the Kingdom of Buyeo came and presented a deer with three antlers and a long-tailed rabbit.

The day of the first full moon festival of the spring of the fifty-third year, the envoy of the Kingdom of Buyeo came and presented a tiger which was one jang and two cheok long, and had white fur and no tail.

In the ninth month of the fifty-fifth year, in the autumn, the King was hunting south of Jil Mountain and caught a purple roe deer.

In the tenth month, in the winter, a local governor presented a red leopard. Its tail was nine ja long.

—From the Annals of the Reign of King Taejo, Sixth Great King of Goguryeo, as recorded in the *Goguryeo Annals of the Samguk Sagi*

When a protracted drought struck the kingdom, the leaves of every plant wilted down into fine, sharp needles, and their stems bulged, to conserve as much water as possible. Fat collected and grew beneath the horses' skin, and formed into humps on their backs, and squirrels began to build their nests beneath the cool ground instead of in the trees. Dogs, unable to bear the heat, shed their fur in clumps. Even in the fall, the fields turned not golden but a drab green, because people planted potatoes and corn instead of rice.

I always worried because whenever a drought struck, an accursed storm of blood always followed. The king always laid the blame at anyone's feet: government officials had committed some kind of error . . . or the royal *samu* had slacked off during his divination ceremonies . . . or the soldiers had gone lax at their guard-posts. Ever since that torrent of blood first surged out from the heart of the palace, through the front gate and out into the courtyard beyond, all manner of alarming stories had spread. It was rumored that when the king slumbered, he set his head upon a human pillow, and that when he sat, it was likewise upon a person . . . and that if either dared to move, the king would slay them with his sword.

The people call him simply Cha-Daewang, "The Next Great King." *Next,* that is, in relation to his predecessor, Great King Taejo. After the previous king, Taejo, had lain ill in his royal bed for an extended period, he'd delegated authority to Cha-Daewang, who had responded with conspiracy. To claim the throne, he had quoted ancient scriptures: "Traditionally, when the senior brother grew elderly, his younger brother was to succeed to the throne . . ." Great King Taejo, powerless to fight him off and anyway wise enough to desire no further spilling of blood, had abdicated the throne and gone off to live out his last days in seclusion in his detached palace.

Following the accession of the Cha-Daewang, I stayed home, barely going outside. Only into the dark of night, like a bat, did I escape my room, wandering around briefly while trying to avoid others' gaze, and returning home before dawn. My skin turned indigo, matching the hue of the night, and my eyes began to gleam yellow. A physician reassured me that I shouldn't fret over this, for it was, he said, merely a deformation of my retina, an unusual new layer to reflect the light from the back of my eyeballs; and that the development of this odd retinal layer is actually common to people who work at night. He also explained why my pupils stretch inhumanly wide at night, while narrowing during the day time, like a cat's: it was merely to control the quantity of light to which I was exposed. When I worried about whether I might pass this trait on to my children someday, he reassured me, speaking of some theory he called *yong-bul-yong,* that is, use-and-disuse, according to which such traits would be unlikely to be passed down beyond a single generation. There was no evidence, he said, that such "acquired characteristics" would be passed down to later descendants this way.

One hot night, I escaped from my room and headed to one of the royal altars. By then, the *samu* had been performing their fire-rites, in an attempt to summon the rains, for several weeks. One of them—a *samu* I knew and got along with well—noticed me hiding in the darkness, and came over to greet me. We'd known one another since childhood, and were of the same age; now he was the only one remaining who wasn't perpetually bent at the waist. (Our royal subjects had spent so long bent forward deferentially before the king, that now their bodies were warped into a permanent bow, and their faces always pointed toward the ground.)

"What has brought you here so late at night, Your Royal Highness?"

It was precisely on account of situations such as this that I avoided going out in public: despite the status of Tae-ja—the Crown Prince—having transferred from me to my cousin, many people still followed the old habit of referring to me as if it had not. Each time someone committed such an error, it felt as if my life has been palpably shortened by several years.

"I was just dropping by to check in on the rain invocations . . . "

The *samu* glanced around and whispered, "How could the sky not turn dry, when the hearts of the people are so parched? True, it is when the people are fatigued that the sky *ought* to be kindest to them, but nature's laws don't work that way."

"I remember my deceased father often used to call down the rains."

"As you may know, my lord, to summon rain requires a change in atmospheric pressure. For example, when one's spiritual energies are quickly extended into the sky, the water vapor in the air above condenses and falls down. It also rains when two massive spirits take form in the heavens and do battle there; or when a giant creature blocks the flow of wind, and the air strikes against its body—this, too, may produce rain. It is great movements such as these, in the air, that are necessary to produce precipitation."

"Like . . . at the moment when a great giant moves?"

"Yes, but there aren't so many of them alive now, and each one keeps such a vast territory for itself, because they're so enormous, and such ravenous eaters besides. Your late father was close friends to one such giant, who lived in the Taebek mountains. He used to summon the rains through that Revered Ban-go, but it's been ages since He stirred. They say his body is blanketed with dirt and trees, and that he is now indistinguishable from the bedrock beneath him. Rumor has it the other titans are all in a similarly torpid state, now: to seek them out would be pointless."

The learned had urged for all the current scholars of phylogeny and embryonic recapitulation to gather and study together, for a generation or so, in order to analyze the rules governing the differentiation of living things. Even so, since all the forms of everything living will have metamorphosed within a generation, such study is pointless. Many such scholars have declared, "There exists no rule governing the differentiation of forms," and retreated to their beds, concealing themselves beneath their blankets. But a certain tendency definitely exists. Most giants who lived during prehistory have ceased in every life-function, including breathing and movement, and chosen to become mountains, rivers, and lakes. Likewise, the tremendous lizards which once dwelled on the earth and in the heavens had also cast aside their dignity and diminished themselves to the size of one's finger.

"Is there *any* sign that points to a resurgence of the giants?"

"With so little known about nature's governance of how forms evolve . . . how should I know? Still, it seems unlikely for anything too enormous to reappear. These days, not only humans, but even smaller animals tend to hunt anything too big. That's why lizards have became smaller: coordinated group effort pays off more than the trouble of maintaining a single, vast body."

"So is there *no* other way to call the rain?"

"For now, all we can do is pray. Sure, human longings are unscientific, but . . . that doesn't mean they have no effect."

As I turned to leave, he added one more comment: "I noticed that the sun is due to swallow the moon on the last night of this month. Please be careful: it's inauspicious . . . "

As I watched him return to his place, I pondered about the meaning of his warning. It was a bizarre comment: a lunar eclipse? During the new moon? How could that happen? The moon's face would be hidden from the sky, and anyway, wasn't a lunar eclipse caused when the Earth's shadow darkened the moon? If the sun were to "shade" the moon, would not the night blaze bright as day? But then, gazing up into the night sky as I pondered his words, I realized my error: even on the last night of the lunar month, the moon still hung in the sky—it was merely hidden from view. To what end might the sun swallow and shade the moon, when it is already invisible? Wouldn't that just be mere nonsense, some sort of purposeless cruelty? The sun was the father of all time, as the king is the father of the people; therefore . . . the cruel sun must represent the cruel king . . . and . . . the invisible moon must be the prince who lost his inheritance . . .

I let out a deep sigh. There was no way to prepare myself for that, though I felt no inclination to do so anyway. Even before he'd claimed the throne from my father, my uncle had already held the reins of power. Even street-beggars have a place to lean their backs against, when they want to rest their legs. Me? I have nothing to lean against in this world . . . so how could I sustain my life, even if I did flee?

I crawled through the darkness back to my room. I usually climbed over trees and scuttled over the ground instead of walking on two feet. I first began doing so, bending my body down each time I heard footsteps, to avoid discovery, but at some point a callus had formed upon my palms, like the ones on people's feet.

It has been said since ancient days that ontogeny repeats phylogeny. The cells of our bodies continue being born and dying at every moment, and the blood in our veins is continually being created and disappearing; when old cells die, then new ones appear to fill the gaps left behind, and soon enough, not one of the original cells of one's body remains. In other words, one truly becomes a completely different creature not only in mind, but also in body. All creatures, whether they wish it or no, die and are reborn several times during their lives.

My late mother, bless her, emphasized repeatedly how revolting one's appearance would be at the end of his life, if he failed to spend his whole life struggling ceaselessly to maintain his humanity. Only a rare few manage to die with a recognizably human form: many more people end their lives shaped like animals and insects. The aristocrats who pass their days comfortably in their rooms, living off taxes and stipends garnered from the people, lose their human forms the soonest. How many of them develop stubby legs and tails, and fat, reddish bellies, their faces dominated by bulging cheeks!

From my early childhood, my mother constantly repeated to me the tale of one woodcutter. This woodcutter was married to a woman from a certain winged race whom he met by chance at the shore of a lake, but after his wife flew away into the sky he went up to the roof and wept, and could neither eat nor sleep. His body diminished until it was tiny, and his legs became as thin as chopsticks, while the bottoms of his feet bent and curved, and curved claws sprouted from his toes like the hooks that hold up the bar of a clothes-rack. His fingers atrophied, and then disappeared, while white feathers sprouted all over his body. A scarlet comb grew upon his head and from his throat came the sound of a heartbroken bird, instead of the sound of a man. His longing had transformed his appearance into that of a rooster, but those wings were useless: he could not fly to where his wife had fled. If only his will and longing had been directed more sensibly, he could have developed wings capable of flight, but he had already lost his wits and sealed his fate, by letting slip his ability to control or direct his own development.

People separated from their lovers become flowers, or ossify into stones like the one in the famous story of Mangbuseok, instead of turning into birds or horses. This tendency of creatures to metamorphose into the complete opposite of that which they long to become is also fascinating. Do you realize that the widely-credited notion that sunflowers follow the sun, is actually mere fantasy? They certainly do grow large flowers out of admiration for the sun, but then they bend their faces down toward the ground. They do this because they cannot bear the weight of those flowers. I thought then that perhaps I was like these others: since I wished nothing so much as to flap my wings and fly far away, maybe I would die instead with a heavy body, its belly stuck to the ground as it crawled about.

The rains never came, but a late freeze struck the land that spring. Some birds dropped from the sky, frozen dead, while those that survived grew thick coats of feathers. When the cold snap continued, some fat, flightless birds waddled along the ground. Other birds leaped into the water, finding some slight warmth in its depths. Beast and human alike began to starve, for they couldn't eat even the leaves of the plants, which had long since metamorphosed into thorns. People hid in the mountains and grew long, thick coats of fur, like beasts. Sometimes when people hunted bears, the bears cried out with voices that sounded less ursine than human.

On the spring day that the assassins came for me, a frost had appeared overnight in the yard outside my home. I was sitting in my room when I noticed some people hiding at a distance behind the trees and walls, quietly approaching my detached palace. Their careful, secretive movements were so furtive that to watch them and wait practically bored me. Before the assassins arrived, my eunuch entered the room and threw himself upon the floor before me.

"Your Royal Highness, the king's assassins are approaching the palace," he told me. "Please, you must flee quickly!"

"To where? My uncle rules this whole land," I replied calmly, flipping the pages of my book. For some reason, the eunuch began to weep.

He sobbed for a while before raising his head, and dutifully said, "Nobody will recognize you, since your appearance has changed so drastically! Let us exchange clothes, so that the Royal Body may survive their attack!" Afterward, he pushed me toward the back door, and sat himself down upon my seat. The night was chilly, and as I crawled out into the dark courtyard, shadowy figures raced into my room. Then the slashing of swords and screaming voices assailed me from behind.

Grief-stricken, I reflected sorrowfully that my father had founded a nation, and won glory in the eyes of the world's, but I, his foolish son, could only crawl about on four legs and stay alive by wretchedly allowing another to die in his place. Suddenly death terrified me, for how could I face my father in the next world?

At that instant came a clap of thunder, and a shower of rain commenced, extinguishing all the torches and plunging the palace into darkness. Finally, at just the right moment, the prayers of the *samu* had reached heaven. Although it was surely a coincidence, the palace soldiers, ignorant of the sciences, fled in terrified confusion, certain that their own misdeeds had angered the heavens. I seized that instant to go over the palace wall. A lone soldier caught sight of me, but on account of my glowing yellow eyes, he must have supposed I was just some cat upon the wall.

I couldn't bear the thought of being around people, so made for the mountains. The rain, having broken the drought, was met by grass surging forth, each blade raising its head toward the sky, and trees unfolding their leaves, while greedily stretching out their roots. In my footsteps, patches of verdant grass sprouted and sank back down toward the soil. The drought, and the sudden rain, had provoked from the plants this animalistic behavior: since it was uncertain when it might rain again, the whole forest around me was noisily occupied spreading seed and growing fruit. I walked and walked through the downpour, until I could walk no more and dropped to the ground in exhaustion.

There I lay, for I don't know how long, until I caught a groggy glimpse of what looked like a white birch tree moving. But when I opened my eyes more widely, and looked carefully, I realized it was no birch at all, but a white tiger. The beast was only a foot tall, slender and tailless, and all its body as white as fresh snow. The tiger crept quietly around me. I remained supine, lacking the strength to flee the creature, and with a wan smile I wondered whether it was a worthy death, to join the cycle of sustenance in the form of a predator's meal.

"What's so funny?"

When the tiger spoke, I was stunned. Its voice was very clear, with exacting and altogether *human* pronunciation. How could a tiger speak a human language with such different vocal cords? Momentarily, I let out an anxious laugh, and tears—just then inexplicable to me—fell from my eyes.

The tiger spoke again, asking, "Why do you weep?"

"I cried because I feel such pity for you," I said, remaining where I lay.

The tiger laughed . . . *human* laughter. "What's so piteous about me?"

"If you can speak human languages, it means you have a human mind; and if you have a human mind, you once were human, despite your present, animal form. I don't how you came to take the shape of a beast, but it's sad, isn't it? How could it not be pitiful, to lose that original form which you inherited from your parents?"

"What does *original form* mean, anyway? Ought every creature to spend its whole life as a newborn infant?" the tiger quipped. "You say you were born in a human form, but your ancestors were once bears and tigers, snakes and fishes, and birds and plants. Now you fight to hang onto this human shape, but ultimately you'll realize the effort is pointless. What's so precious about dying in the same form you were born into? I might look like an animal, but I chose this form: I *wanted* to fill my belly with the work of my own two hands . . . and this form is the result."

I had nothing to offer in reply.

"Do you know that in the old days," it continued, "it took aeons for creatures to change from one form to another; that it took many ten-thousands of aeons for any kind of differentiation at all to develop. Things aren't better or worse now—it's just that a different kind of adaptation is necessary these days. Nature chooses its survivors without considering good, or evil, or superior, or inferior. Even the human form is just a single means of survival chosen by nature. Humans are frailer than rabbits, when they're not in a group or deprived of their tools! A pathetic weakling like you . . . pitying me? How insolent!"

The tiger bared its razor-sharp fangs at me, its wrath apparent, so I shut my eyes and tensed in anticipation of the coming attack . . . but as long as I waited, it didn't slash open my throat. When I dared to open my eyes, I found the tiger quietly watching me.

"Say it," the creature finally said.

"Say what?"

"What is it you *want*?"

"I don't want *anything*," I said. "I just don't want to be discovered by anyone. I want to live and die without anyone finding me."

The tiger said, "You should become a bug, then. Since you can't get over this fixation on people, it'd be best to become a maggot or a fly. Or . . . how about a worm? Worms enrich the soil. You'd be more useful to people that way, than whatever it is you are right now."

Though every single word he spoke dripped with insult, I couldn't think of any suitable rejoinder to offer him.

"But those forms *are* rather distant from mine," I said. "Becoming a worm would probably be *really* difficult. What can I do?"

"If you really, *truly* wanted to dig holes and eat dirt, it wouldn't be *so* hard, now, would it?" the tiger retorted. Then it looked up at me, and said, "Well, I can't eat someone I've had a conversation with, so you go on back, now. I saw some starving people climbing up the mountain: if you follow them, you might even learn how to survive out here . . ."

Then he departed through the trees, blending into the background until his silhouette suddenly disappeared from view.

I rose from the ground.

After following the mountain ridge for a while, I encountered the group of climbers the tiger had described. I joined them, blending in as best I could; not a soul in the group addressed me, or even seemed to notice me—or pay attention to one another, for that matter. Nobody even commented on my indigo skin or my xanthous eyes. Among them were folk with folded spines, twisted faces, legless or armless, carapaced like sea-creatures, or crawling upon four feet.

The climbers eventually split into threes and fives and entered a series of caves. When I followed them inside, I found people lying asleep in one anothers' arms. They seemed to have chosen to hibernate through the cold, barren years, rather than starve. Some spun cocoons, silkworm-like, and others grew thin membraneous coverings, like the diaphanous skin that bundles fishes' eggs together. There were also people covered with coats of white fur. Those who couldn't change so quickly, or handle such a rapid metamorphosis, died and became prey to the ants, joining the cycle of digestion and nutriment to live on in a different form within that cycle. I tried to find a spot empty of people, and finally settled between the roots at the foot of a great tree. I gathered grass around me and fashioned a bed from it, and then I rolled myself around and attempted to hibernate.

Winter came, and my starvation continued. Struggling, I attempted to subsist on soil alone, but I couldn't do it. I tried to hibernate, but always woke; now sleeping, now waking again. Eventually, I was able to sleep for a few days in a row, then four, and finally I was able to slumber for a week to ten days at a time.

During the winter I shed my skin. My body, failing under the hardships of my new environment, seemed of its own accord to have decided that some sort of "adjustment" was necessary: radical changes occurred in my skeletal structure and the placement of my vital organs. I passed out and woke again several times more, as my skin fell from my flesh. When I finally climbed out from my moult, and looked back, the ghastly husk still looked all too horribly human. As for me, I found I had grown a smooth, serpent-like skin and a long lizard's tail. I wept briefly for my lost humanity, but soon I regained my calm. My body had taken this reptilian form in order to best ensure my survival, I supposed: the wisdom of the flesh outweighs all the reason of the human mind. It understands that survival is more crucial than a man's dignity or pride. I turned and devoured my abandoned human skin, a feast of precious nutriment for my new body.

When spring arrived, and edible grass began to sprout at the mouth of the cave, I woke up from my slumber and crept outside. Then, I realized that I was the only one who had survived from this long, terrible winter. A few others had perished outside, taking the form of human-shaped rocks and trees, all entangled together in a solemn tableau. Respectfully, I performed a ceremony before them: they, at least, were noble enough to prefer becoming soil to losing their human shape.

After that, I dwelled in the forest, crawling upon the ground and eating grass. My jaw soon became powerful, the better to chew on the tough grass, and I developed a sort of jutting snout, as well. My ears grew pointed, because of how I pricked them up at every swaying of the brush nearby, and my palms hardened as my limbs shortened to suit my body. When I could no longer use my fingers, horns sprouted from my skull; they began as small nubs on my head, but soon it branched out like the antlers of a male deer. These horns were invaluable in the battles I fought with other beasts over food, and for striking trees to coax them into reluctantly letting drop their ripe fruit.

In the winter of that year, I shed my skin once more. I discovered my entire body to have completely changed to the dull greenish color of the forest. I wondered whether living in a desert, or on a rocky mountain, might perhaps help me to maintain my human pigmentation, but the proposition seemed useless to me. My desire to go unseen was so great that my body would surely be inscribed with the camouflaging patterns of the pebbles, if I lived upon a rocky mountain.

I looked down at the little nub that remained, down below my belly button, and wondered whether I could even still have sex with a human being. The thought made me laugh and laugh. Even though my bestial transformation was past the point of no return, still I couldn't abjure this strange wistfulness for my own long-lost form. But someday my brain, too, would undergo its own transformation in capacity and structure. How much longer would I retain my very consciousness, my memories and human intellect? That night, I counted the number of scales that had grown upon my body, and found them—counting both the great and the small ones together—to number eighty-one. *The square of nine,* I thought: *That's a lucky number.*

After that thought, I began to laugh once more.

· · ·

I think it was probably autumn.

While crawling through the forest as always in search of food, I heard the distant din of horseshoes and barking hounds. When I looked up in surprise, a group of hunting dogs was chasing a small group of purple roe deer toward me. I fled as swiftly as I could, amid the rushing deer, but the hunters mistook me for one of them, on account of my antlers and loosed their arrows at me. One poor deer, struck by an arrow beside me, rolled on the ground and screamed piteously. Its voice was so very human that my heart all but failed me.

Although I ran myself half-dead, I was neither so fleet nor so clever as the rest of the herd. Eventually, I ended up surrounded by hunting hounds, at the foot of a great tree and unable to move. As I stood there, buffeted by the baying and barking of the hounds, the bushes split apart and people armed with arrows and spears appeared. I stood frozen as I watched a man on horseback leading them forward.

His face had haunted me everywhere but in my dreams: it was my own uncle. But that wasn't the reason that I couldn't move or speak. *That* was because of his incredible appearance, which had changed so drastically that he was unrecognizable.

He looked like a giant hunk of meat.

His bulging pink gut shone with his gluttony, and his peaked nose signified a lifetime with his face buried in food. His almost-shut eyes reflected a near-absolute lack of moral discernment within, and the upward curve of his earlobes, covering his ears completely, reflected his desire to hear nothing at all. The spaces between his fingers had disappeared, because his hands and feet had atrophied, meaning he had attended to none of his royal tasks. Considering how my late father had retained his human appearance even during his prolonged sickness in bed, my uncle's transformation was truly outrageous. I was simply too shocked and outraged to fear him.

My uncle directed them to lower their arrows from me, and examined me from snout to tail.

"What is this beast? Because of the antlers, I thought it was a deer, but its body is such a nasty shade of green. The thing has the tail of a lizard and is covered with scales like a snake's . . . its arms and legs are like a human's, but its yellow eyes look like a cat's. What kind of an omen might this be?"

A servant hurried forth to his side. His back was bent, as if he were slumped upon on a horse's back, and his neck bent groundward, as if we were about to topple over at any moment. His appearance had undergone a profound transformation, but I recognized him then as the *samu* who had once been my true friend. I sensed that he recognized me, too, though he was fighting to look away from me.

"It's not unusual to encounter new kinds of creatures, since animals constantly change, adjusting to their environment. However, the reason lineage is so very unstable is because of the instability of this *world* in which the subjects of Your Majesty live. Nature presents us with monstrosities like this because it cannot communicate its earnest mind with words . . . which is to renew itself by filling the king with fear and regret. But, if the king cultivates his virtue, this unfortunate omen can be transformed to a lucky one."

The listening king's face quietly turned scarlet.

"If it's unpropitious, just tell me that. Or if it is propitious, then tell me *that*. Telling me it's an ill omen, but then claiming it *could* be a good one . . . what sort of a lie is that?"

Before anyone around could stop the king, he drew the sword at his waist. The sword swayed about, lopping off the heads of the *samu* and the others near him. Just then, I turned tail and fled. Behind me, innumerable arrows fell amid the barking of the hounds, and I scrambled up the mountain for dear life. When I finally reached a cliff, I looked down at the mighty, meandering river and leaped from the precipice.

When I struck the water from such a height, I found it as hard as the ground would have been. The river gulped me down whole.

I learned several facts. One cannot gain wings by jumping down from a cliff only once, and one can't die easily when one's body is covered with unexpectedly hard reptilian skin.

I had hoped so fervently to live without being discovered by people, but when that happened, again someone had died.

After that, I stayed in the river. My skin, after soaking in the water for so long, festered and began to grow limp, freezing in the cold of the night. This almost killed me several times, but I didn't dare go back up and onto land. I sincerely hoped that the last strand of my human will might break. I hoped to become a fish or a water snake, and prayed that my human consciousness might be finally drawn out from me completely.

In the middle of the night, while I lay in the glacially-cold shallows, two turtles poked their heads out from the water simultaneously. When they finally surfaced, I realized they weren't two creatures, but one turtle with two heads. It must have burrowed into the muddy bed of the river, because it was almost two *cheok* tall, all told. Fish with red wings flopped and scooted away from it.

"Why does this land creature shove its head into the water this cold night? It should go back to where it came from," the turtle said, its voice seeming to echo as the two heads spoke out in unison.

I opened my frozen mouth to reply: "I have nowhere to go. If I've intruded on your territory, I sincerely apologize, but please don't cast me out."

"Every creature has its territory . . . but why would a four-legged beast try to live by breathing water?"

"If we're arguing about origins, there are no strict boundaries in lineage. If you'll admit that your own form and character includes setting foot in both soil *and* water, then you of all creatures will recognize that all land-creatures once dwelt in water. Recall: every creature derives from a single origin. If dolphins and sea lions are blameless, then how is it that I warrant criticism, even if I'm simply trying to retrace my way back to our origins?"

"Well, there might be no borders, but a weirdo like you wandering around here is sure to make my prey panic and flee . . . "

"I didn't mean to . . . I only sought to escape discovery by others, but that seems hopeless. But I am anxious to discuss this tendency of creatures to develop an appearance contrary to their desires . . . to share a few days' discussion on the subject, perhaps . . . "

"There's no *need* for a few days' discussion. It's simple: you just don't really want what you think you want." The turtle thrust its two heads toward me, crossing them, and snapped, "Now, scram. If you don't, I'll eat you up."

"Go ahead and eat me," I replied. "After I die, I'll become a water-ghost, and never walk on land again." Then I shut my eyes.

When I opened them again a while later, the turtle was gone. Perhaps it hadn't killed me out of sympathy, or because it wasn't worth the effort . . . or maybe I just didn't look very appetizing? I braced myself to bear the watery chill throughout the remainder of the night.

After some more time passed, the scales upon my skin grew affixed to their places, and my arms and legs diminished gradually, growing tiny. However, somehow they didn't become fins, but ceased their transformation when they had assumed an avian shape. (I suspected this might have resulted from my leaping into the air from the precipice.) When my arms and legs ceased functioning, my spine and tail stretched longer. It is said that every stage you pass through leaves its indelible mark. Well, the antlers sprouting from my skull didn't atrophy, and remained; and so did the cat's-eyes I'd developed so early in my youth, unchanged even now. To learn to breathe water was insuperable, but

I did learn to dive for extended periods. And as my arms and legs atrophied further, my beard grew longer and developed a sensitivity like that of insects' feelers. I lived by feeding on small fish and water plants. I sank to the bottom of the river for days at a time, and lingered in the lake for several months.

One day, as I rose to the surface to breathe, I came upon a woman doing her laundry. Aside from her nine white tails, she retained a wholly human appearance. I looked at her, uncertain what to do because it had been so long since I'd seen a human being, or worn a human form myself. Seeing her gaze upon me vacantly, I waited for her to scream, to call me a monster and begin to hurl stones at me, but instead she clasped her hands together and bowed deeply before me.

"What're you doing?" I asked her.

I realized my mistake as I opened my mouth. Just as with the tiger, this woman would realize that somewhere in my lineage, there lay hidden a human stage.

"When the Mystical One came out from the water," she said, "I saw that It ruled these waters, so I bowed."

"You saw wrong. I'm just a profane thing, a parasite in these waters, hiding scared of the human world. Forgive me, I didn't mean to surprise you."

Then I sank down again to the bottom of the lake.

Several days later, I opened my eyes and discovered some rice-cakes and fruit, water-logged in the depths before me. Little fish rose toward each sinking rice-cake, nibbling upon them. I rose to the surface once more. The nine-tailed woman I'd met before remained by the lake, but glancing about, I saw that she had set blessed water, incense, and a plate of rice-cakes upon a little wooden table, performing an earnest little ceremony while offering devout prayers. Red papers inscribed with petitions drooped from the table, and several more people, perhaps her neighbors, were gathered around her. When she saw me, she leaped up like a thief caught red-handed.

I balked, stupefied. "What's all this shit? Didn't I tell you with my own mouth? I'm nothing more than a mongrel! If you have nowhere to hold your ceremony, go to another lake, or a mountain instead!"

She said, "The trees are desiccated, and the drought has gone on so long; the grassroots folk have barely any way to find themselves food. Everything is growing and changing so strangely, our farms are falling apart, and our harvests no longer suit the people's diets. And the king can't hear us: his ears and eyes have atrophied."

"So what do you want from me? I have no power. How can a beast get involved in human affairs?"

"There must be *some* reason why nature has allowed you such a sacred appearance . . . but, are you saying everything we humans have hoped for is in vain?"

I shut my mouth for a moment, before saying, "What you say is correct."

I swung my tail, which sent a blast of wind and raised a spray of water, knocking down the incense and sending the bowl of holy water tumbling, to break upon the ground.

Then I said, "Oh, how long I have lived . . . and every time anyone discovers me, I bring trouble. It's better I never show myself again."

I sank down into the depths once more. When I looked back up, I saw the nine-tailed woman weeping. Cold-bloodedly, I turned my head away, nestling myself into the bottom of the lake, and began to hibernate. The frigid water began to freeze my body, its functions slowing gradually, paralyzing me, until I could feel each of my cells passing into a kind of slumber. I no longer felt the passage of time, and my thoughts slowed. I thought, if I was lucky, I might transmute into rock, or soil—like the giants of ancient days.

At first, it felt like someone knocking on a distant door, but then it became a voice, trying to stir me: "Wake up."

I opened my eyes. It was difficult to do so: a host of water plants and marsh snails had attached themselves to my body. But then I saw the two-headed turtle, whom I'd met before, swimming before my own eyes. Somehow he looked much smaller than before.

"Leave. Soon. The king's army is here to catch you."

I needed a moment to comprehend his words. Then, I recalled that I'd once, long ago, been a human being . . . and a prince . . . and I recalled my blood-relation to the king then, too.

"Why would the king bother to come and catch me?"

"Even after you began to sleep, the people continued their ceremonies here. They were praying to you to expel the king and bring them a new one, so he decided to fill in the lake and dig you out from the bottom. Your mind is so slow now; your brain must have metamorphosed. Get out of here, *now*."

In fact, I was surrounded by a din of noise. When I raised my head up, clod after clod of soil fell upon my head. From somewhere came the revolting stink of blood, and a murder of crows were coming and going in a chaos over the lake.

"Why the crows are squawking like that?"

"It's really dreadful. Better you don't see it," the turtle said, and then he burrowed into the mud.

I rose to the surface, in an ominous mood. Even my slightest movement stirred up a whirlpool, sending fish fleeing in surprise. A multitude of water plants and marsh snails dropped from my body. Then, I realized that the turtle hadn't become smaller; perhaps because of my long slumber, I had become *bigger*.

A band of soldiers were gathered near the lakeshore, dumping soil into the water. When they saw me they fell into shocked silence, and ceased shoveling. I also lost my words, and looked at the things embedded in the mud around them: the dead bodies of the villagers who'd held the ceremonies, and the woman lay in a terrible row beside the lake. The nine-tailed woman's white underskirts flapped back and forth in the breeze, and with each flap of the fabric my reason fell away a little, until finally my mind had gone blank.

One of the soldiers came to his senses and roared at me, waving his spear: "You freakish beast, bare your neck to us tamely! All your followers are dead!"

Before he even finished his words, I sprang up from the water, and then I bit through a soldier nearby, in the front rank, with my fangs; while the men roiled in confusion, I struck their horses' legs with my tail. I tore at the throats of the fallen with my claws, and as they groaned I crushed their hearts with my two front paws. When I heard the noise of distant soldiers, too, I fled the lake and leaped into the river. My eyes had always been sharp, and I was able to count the dead by the riverside, one by one. Then I saw the man who had once been my uncle, standing near the river. I tried to slip past him, but then I heard his voice: "Come here, you phantasm!"

The king sat straight-backed upon a horse, and spoke in such a tiny voice, though for me, having gone through so many bestial transformations, his voice was crystal clear. He said, "If you don't come out, I'll kill everyone in the village until I catch you. I'll accuse them of worshipping a spirit-monster and execute them all!"

I stopped swimming. It was a bizarre threat. Even my uncle thought that I retained some shred of sacred compassion within me. What relation had I with the lives and deaths of mere human beings? Yet I emerged from the water quietly, going up to the edge of the river, and stood before the king. Of course, it was impossible for my body to *stand up* like a human does, but I coiled my long tail in a spiral to support my body and hold my neck upright. When I stood myself up thus, I realized how immense I'd become. The soldiers with their spears pointing up at me, and my uncle, they all looked so puny that I could sweep them away in an instant.

A thousand emotions flooded me as I regarded my uncle closely. Ah, ah . . . he'd gotten old. That transformation must be the end of any creature, even the one that resists any change at all. His once fat belly drooped with wrinkles, his creased face was blotched, and his atrophied arms and legs had dried out in their disuse, and thinned extremely.

"Now, I recognize you," he said with very dry voice, like branches rasping in the wind. "You are the seed of the former king. The seed that should've dried out long before still remains . . . "

I bowed my head, imitating his soldiers who had bent their heads, facing down, and said, "The reason this insignificant one became a beast is not to threaten Your Majesty's rule, but only to sustain its own existence. These acts were committed by the ignorant, so I beg that you please temper your rage with your vast generosity."

"You say it's an act of ignorance, but you must have known what they were doing, so I have no choice but to accuse you of your crime."

"This flesh lost its old life ages ago; why are you trying to take that life twice?"

"How dare you speak and act that way toward your king?" demanded the king with a piercing voice as thin as a eunuch, so thin I could barely hear it. "Since you are in my kingdom, your body and life are mine. I demand that you to bestow your life to me, as a dutiful subject. *Obey my command.*"

"What on earth do you want with the life of a worthless water snake?"

"How dare a beast converse with a man? How insolent, how disrespectful! You're such a vile portent! I'm going to conquer you, and get rid of you."

"This insignificant one may have become a wicked beast, but the king is no longer human either. How can you demand my life, while pretending at being the king of the humans?"

The corners of the King's blind eyes twisted upward with his fury. As he cried out in that thin voice of his, soldiers all around ran toward me, while kicking their horses into action. I dived into the river again. The soldiers chased me along the riverbank, and I swam like the wind, so quickly that the river overflowed and the waters parted behind me.

I heard the laughter of the king suddenly from behind. I knew the reason of his laughing. A great waterfall, ten *jang* tall, blocked the way up ahead. However, instead of stopping I pushed myself harder. When I reached the bottom of the waterfall, I threw myself upward, stealing momentum from the whirlpool at its base, and leapt up the falls. My body ascended past the falling water, and the whirlpool that encircled my tail also swirled and rose up with me.

I realized that I had generated an ascending wind, and that my body had become so gigantic that I could direct the currents of the air. I rose up into the sky, riding that wind, and the soldiers who were chasing me stopped to watch, befuddled. As I examined my body, I found my greenish scales shimmering spectacularly in the sunlight, and my long tail swung behind me, almost as if to touch the ground. I felt wonderful, so I continued to ascend higher. The air current was practically visible to me, almost palpable, and I sensed how I could change my direction by riding the wind. I realized, then, how to shift the flowing air currents in order to produce rain. Recalling the past, I remembered hating droughts during my human days, though that had been so long ago I couldn't quite remember quite.

I directed the air currents upward. Dark clouds formed as soon as the water vapor in the air was carried up into the troposphere. Suddenly, the world was shaken by lightning and thunder. When I shifted the pressure of the air by pressing the clouds gently and then rising up, a heavy rain began to pour toward the ground. The river flooded, the fields deluged, and in a flash the waters swept away the distracted soldiers who stood near the riverbanks, watching me overhead. Powerless to pursue me, the king watched from a distance; immediately his hair whitened and he seemed to turn a decade older in an instant. It was as if I'd evaporated away the last bit of life left in him. However, their lives and deaths interested me not at all, for I was no longer human. It was in skimming the clouds that I exulted, so I built up speed and began to rise steadily higher.

That was that winter the king died in an uprising. That was the day when I soared through an azure sky.

Originally published in Korean in *HappySF,* Volume 2, 2006.

ABOUT THE AUTHOR

Kim Bo-young is one of South Korea's most active and important SF authors. Her first published work of fiction, a novella titled "The Experience of Touch" (2002), received the award for best novella in the first round of the Korean Science & Technology Creative Writing Awards in 2004. Since then, she has published numerous works of short fiction in assorted Korean SF anthologies and magazines. In 2010 she published a two-volume collection of short stories, *The Story Goes That Far* and *An Evolutionary Myth*. 2013 saw the publication of her first novel, *The Seven Executioners,* which won the first annual South Korean SF novel award (a prize launched in 2014). Kim enjoys widespread popularity and support among Korean SF fandom, and on the strength of her fiction writing, she was recruited by Bong Joon-ho to serve as a script advisor during the development of his film *Snowpiercer.* She lives in Gangwon Province, South Korea with her family, and continues to write while operating a farm that produces peppers and chillies.

Solace

JAMES VAN PELT

The wall display didn't last two sleep cycles. When Meghan woke the first time, one hundred years into the four thousand years long journey to Zeta Reticula, she waved her hand at the sensor, and the steel wall morphed into a long view of the Crystal River. On the left side, aspen leaves trembled in a breeze she couldn't feel. The river itself cut across the image, appearing between trees, tumbling over rocks, chuckling and hissing through the speakers before draining onto the floor at the bottom of the image. On the river's right bank, the generator house, a remnant of 19th Century mining, clung to a gray granite outcrop. A tall water chute dropped from the building's bottom, down the short cliff to a pool below. She'd taken the picture on her last hike before reporting for flight training. Every crew member's room had a display. Only hers showed the same scene continuously. She joined the crew for their fourteen-day work period, and then returned to the long-sleep bed.

But when she awoke the second time, two hundred years after they left Earth orbit, the metal wall remained grimly blank. She sat on her bunk's edge, empty, knowing the lead in her limbs was the result of a hundred years of sleep but believing that sadness caused it. No mountain. No river. No rustic generator house standing against the aspen. She called for Crew Chief Teague.

While she waited, she opened the box under her bed where she kept a souvenir from Earth, a miner's iron candlestick holder, a long spike at one end, a brass handle on the other, and a metal loop in the middle to hold the candle. She'd found it in a pit beside the generator house after she'd taken the picture. It had a nice heft to it, balanced in her hand. She had cleaned the rust off so the metal shined, but pits marred what must have at one time been a smooth surface. She liked the roughness under her fingers.

After checking the circuits, crew chief Teague said, "Everything about this expedition is an experiment." He punched at the manual overrides for the display behind a cover plate in Meghan's room. "There's no way to test the effects of time on technology except to watch it over time, and that's what we're doing." He clicked the plate shut. "All that matters is keeping life support, guidance, and propulsion running for the whole trip. You make sure hydroponics continue to function. I work in mechanical repair. Teams service the power plant. One of the four crews is awake every twenty-five years, but we don't have time to repair a luxury like your display wall. We're janitors." He ran his hand down the blank surface. "It's already an old ship, and we have a long, long way to go."

"*We* have to keep running too. The people."

"Yes, there is that." He rubbed his chin while looking at the candlestick holder in her lap. "Interesting piece. Does the handle unscrew?"

She twisted it. "Seems stuck."

"We could open in the machine shop."

She shook her head.

After Teague left, Meghan tried to remember how the river looked and sounded. With the wall display working, she could imagine an aspen breeze on her face, the rushing water's pebbly smell. She could remember uneven ground, slickness of spray-splashed rocks, stirred leaves' sweetness. With eyes closed, she tried to evoke the memory. Hadn't the ground been a little slippery with gravel? Hadn't there been a crow circling overhead? When she was a little girl, her mother died. A month later Meghan could not remember her Mom's face. Only after digging into a scrapbook did the sense of her mother come back to her. Now, it was just as bad, but what she couldn't remember was Earth. The metal walls, the synthetic cushioning on the floor, the ventilation's constant hiss seemed like they had been a part of her forever, and the Earth slipped away, piece by piece.

She placed the flat of her hand on the blank wall. It's only two years, she thought. In two years I'll be out of the ship, if the planet around Zeta Reticula is habitable. But she shivered. Only two *subjective* years. She'd spend most of the trip in the long-sleep cocoon. If the technology worked, she would leave the ship in four thousand real years.

Teague was right, though, about untested technology. Nearly every element of the expedition was a prototype. Could a human-manufactured device continue to function after four thousand years, even with constant maintenance? The Egyptian pyramids were forty-five hundred years old, and they still stood, but they were merely rocks in a pile, not a sophisticated space vehicle. After four thousand years, the pyramids weren't expected to enter an orbit around a distant planet while maintaining a sustainable environment against the deadliness of space.

And what of the people on board? The only test of the technology that kept a person alive for four thousand years and preserved the seeds and fertilized ova would take four thousand years. Dr. Arnold, who knew all their medical charts by heart, told her that what she felt was homesickness. Like Meghan and the rest of the crew, he was in his twenties, but he spoke with maturity. Meghan trusted him. "Look for these symptoms," he said, "episodic or constant crying, nausea, difficulty sleeping, disrupted menstrual cycle." He consulted his notes. "Of course, those symptoms may also be induced by long sleep." His assistant, Dr. Singh, nodded in agreement.

"Dr. Arnold, I'm two hundred years late on my last period."

Already she felt old. Already, with the sun no more than a bright star in their wake, she felt creaky and removed, a part of the dead. I shouldn't be able to sense Earth's pull from here, she thought. I shouldn't have come. They should have known that a hydroponics officer wouldn't do well away from Earth, away from forests and long stretches of mountain grass. Even when we arrive, if everything works, if the planet is hospitable, it will take years and years to grow Earth trees to sit beneath. I'll never see an aspen again.

I won't make it.

Isaac scooted his stool closer to the tiny woodstove. If he sat close enough, long enough, the warmth crept through his mittens and the arms of his coat. His knees, only a few inches from the stove, nearly blistered, but the cold pressed against his back. It slipped around the sides of his hood. He eyed the tiny pile of wood by the stove, the remains of the table he'd broken into pieces the day before. All the cabin's goods sat on the floor since he'd burned the shelves earlier. Beside the remains of the table, the only other wood was a small box of kindling in case the fire went out, and the chair he sat on. Outside, snow covered the ground so deeply that there was no hope of finding deadfall. Besides, every tree within a mile had either been cut down for mine timbers or had its low branches cut off for firewood. He'd hauled the wood he'd been burning for the last ten days from a site four miles upstream, but that was long before the storm moved in, cutting visibility to a few feet.

In the room below, machinery thumped steadily. Water poured through a sluice to turn a wheel connected to a squat generator. Cables ran up the mountain to the mines' compressors, clearing dead air from the tunnels and powering the drills, but Isaac couldn't tell if the miners were still working. They probably were hunkered down like he was, in their bunk houses near the digging, or they were stuck in the town of Crystal. If they were working, the compressors needed to run.

He looked out the window. Thick frost coated the inside of the glass and snow piled half way up outside dimmed what light the dark afternoon offered. The window in his tiny, second story maintenance room was at least fifteen feet above the ground. Two weeks of non-stop snow had nearly buried the building. Ten days ago, when the supplies clerk dropped off a bag full of dried meat and two loaves of bread, he'd said, "First winter in the mountains, boy? It'll get so cold your piss will freeze before it splashes your boots."

Isaac hadn't been able to open the outside door for the last three days. Heavy snow blocked it. He rubbed his mittens together, trying to distribute the heat. A steady wind moaned outside. Trees creaked. Something snapped sharply overhead. He glanced at the thick timbers supporting the roof. How much weight could they hold? How much crushing snow lay above him?

He sighed, unwilling to leave the stove's meager heat, but he had a job to do. Checking for candles in his coat pocket, he walked down to the darkness of the generator room, a "Tommie Sticker" in hand to hold the light. It was a fancy one, with a brass match holder and a screw-on cap to keep the matches dry serving as the handle. Ice covered the stairs, and the air smelled wet and cold. He jammed the spike end of the Tommie Sticker into the plank wall, then carefully lit the candle, using both hands to hold the match steady against his shivering. Oil for the lamp had run out two days ago. The wavering candle revealed water pounding through the sluice against the horizontal wheel, turning it ponderously counter-clockwise.

Isaac used a two-pond hammer and chisel to clear ice from the water's entrance and exit points. If the machinery stopped, miners would be without ventilation or power. Ice blocks as big as his head broke free from the structure and clattered to the unlevel floor, where they slid to the far wall. Despite the cold, he soon built up a sweat. He pulled his hood back and unfastened the coat's top. When he finished, he would strip his coat and layers of shirts, replacing the damp undershirt with a dry one. If he didn't, he'd be too cold to sleep later.

The work wasn't unlike living in the monastery, he thought, complete with a vow of silence and constant labor to keep his hands busy. He thought about God and God's plan. He never felt as close to heaven as he did when he worked alone, cut off from human conversation and the daily distractions. In a way, he hoped the storm would hold. As long as the weather cut him off, he could replicate life in the monastery. He had loved his room there. The rough-hewn bed and the blanket thrown over a thin mattress. He'd read by candlelight there, too. Yes, the generator house reminded him of the monastery. The wooden building felt like a cradle of the miraculous, a miracle that never occurred when he had been an initiate.

It hadn't been this cold, though. No, not nearly so cold at all.

Meghan came awake slowly and in pain. Dr. Arnold had decided four cycles ago that the powerful painkillers they used to soften the shift from the long sleep's near death to full wakefulness were damaging, so they didn't flood her system with them before they woke her. Lying as still as she could in the cocoon, her elbows and knees ached, as did her ankles and wrists. Even her knuckles hurt. A tear squeezed out of each eye and raced into her ears as she thought about clenching her fists for the first time on her own in a hundred years. Every move would hurt, at first, even though the mechanical manipulators flexed her joints daily.

When she'd gone to sleep last, Crew Chief Teague had refused. She'd shaken his hand before heading to her cocoon. "I'll be okay," he said. "I'll have a rich and long life, working in the ship. In twenty-five years I'll greet the next work crew."

"I'll never see you again," said Meghan.

"Maybe you will. I'll be old though." He didn't meet her eyes. "I can't face the dark."

Meghan could say nothing to that because she understood. Each time, climbing into the cocoon seemed like entering death. A one hundred year long instant later she woke to pain. Even her skin hurt, the now active cells firing neurons back and forth, renewing contacts that had laid moribund for so long, but as she lay in the cocoon this time, she thought about Teague wandering through the ship, all the crews sleeping, and he would wander for years and years and years, twenty-five of them completely alone until the next crew woke, and what could he say to them? He'd have a quarter of a century of experience that none of them could share. For them, Earth was only a couple months in their wake. They were still young in all ways except years. Teague would greet them. "Hi," he might say. "I'm what you will be someday." In him, they'd watch their mortality.

Then, he'd wait twenty-five more years, alone, if he lived, and as an elderly man, he would welcome the next crew to their two weeks of busy wakefulness.

It was unlikely he would meet a third crew. He would be ninety-seven years old, and despite what he said, he certainly would not be alive when she awoke.

She had closed her eyes as the cocoon's lid came down. Her muscles tightened. In a blink, the pain would come, the one hundred year blink. And it did.

It took several hours before she could shuffle to the infirmary. Waking was worse this time. Dr. Arnold said, "We haven't gone a fifth of the way, yet." He massaged her hands, lighting them with a million wincing tingles. "Some of the medical staff may stay awake longer than the two weeks for research." Even though he was young, like her, tiny creases that would become worry lines were evident on his forehead.

She thought his eyes were kind, though. He flinched when she flinched. "Sorry," he said. "I'm trying to be gentle."

When Meghan reached her room, she pulled the protective plastic off her bed and found a fragile note folded on her pillow from Crew Chief Teague, who wrote, "Try the wall now." He had signed and dated it twenty years earlier. An old man wrote this, she thought.

She waved her hand at the sensor, provoking a cascade of pain down her side. The wall flickered. The speakers whispered. Then the Crystal River winked into existence. Water burbled over rocks. Leaves rasped against each other. A long cloud in the distance slid slowly across a mountaintop.

How long had Teague worked on the wall? A present for a young girl he would never see again.

The speakers popped twice, like a computer chip crunching somewhere and the sound turned off, then the image brightened and washed into a pure white. Meghan shaded her eyes before it too vanished. His repair lasted for ten seconds. How long had he worked on it? She tried to open the service panel, but it remained stubbornly closed. Frustrated, she slapped her hand against it, then grabbed the iron candlestick holder from under the bed. Its sharp end pried the small hatch open. Looking at the circuit board underneath revealed nothing, though. Circuit boards were not her area of expertise. The hatch wouldn't reclose.

Meghan stared at the blank wall for a long time before seeking out Dr. Arnold and his soft, kind hands.

"What is that?" he asked, pointing to the candleholder.

Meghan turned the artifact over in her fingers. She hadn't realized that she still carried it. "It's all I have from Earth. It's a miner's light."

She slept with him for the rest of the two weeks until they returned to the cocoons again. The first time, as she pulled his shirt over his head, he said, "You're going to have to quit calling me Dr. Arnold. My name's Sean."

Once, she woke up, still unfamiliar with Sean's shape, and listened to his breathing in the dark room. If she tried hard, it reminded her of wind through the leaves.

Isaac considered the various forms of meditation. He'd learned to plant a question in his mind, then to spend the day or days or weeks contemplating its implications and meaning. While pondering the question, he would read from the Bible or the many studies in the monastery's library. Meditation was best during his vows of silence. At length, the question would glow in his head, like campfire coals. Now, lying on his bed, squeezing his arms close to his body, trying not to shiver, he considered why God allowed cold. Genesis told him that cold was one of the ways God showed man that the Earth would continue. It said, "While the earth remaineth, seedtime and harvest, and cold and heat, and summer and winter, and day and night shall not cease."

Twice in the night, the roof creaked loudly, the second time dumping a pile of snow onto the floor. Holding the Tommy Sticker high, he could see where a board had broken. He wondered how he could get outside of the generator house to knock snow off the roof, but the wind roared and the window showed no outside light at all now. He wasn't sure if it was day or night. Was such a storm normal? He had no mountain experience. The monastery had been challenging, but it didn't teach him how to survive here. If it had *snowed* for forty days and forty nights for Noah, instead of raining, it could hardly be worse than this.

The Bible wasn't clear on snow. Mostly it appeared in the comparison "white as snow" in a dozen passages. He remembered somewhere the prophets linked it to leprosy. By candle he found the verse in Numbers. Turning the pages with his mittens was impossible, so he shucked them off and put them between his legs to keep them warm. The passage said, "And the cloud departed from off the tabernacle; and, behold, Miriam became leprous, white as snow: and Aaron looked upon Miriam, and, behold, she was leprous." In Exodus he came across Moses turning a rod into a snake and back into a rod again. Then God said to Moses, "Put now thine hand into thy bosom. And he put his hand into his bosom: and when he took it out, behold, his hand was leprous as snow."

Even God didn't like snow.

The roof creaked again, sending another icy spill to the growing pile.

The door wouldn't move. Forcing the weight that rested against it was impossible, so he tried the window and pushed it up. A solid white wall stood revealed. He jabbed a shovel into it, dumped snow on the floor, dug in again. A half hour later, he'd cleared a tunnel to the surface, about a foot above the window. He pushed the snowshoes out the hole and, then climbed after them. The wind slammed into his face when he rolled to the surface, and his arm sank to his armpit when he tried to right himself. Strapping on the broad snowshoes took longer than he wished. Snow worked its way into the top of his shoes, froze into little balls on his gloves and fell down his collar. He couldn't see even to the trees that stood twenty yards away from the generator house. His eyes watered, and his cheeks stung. The air's gray luminosity revealed that it was day, but he could barely tell, nor did it matter.

He had imagined by the height of the snow on the generator house that the river valley would be twenty feet under, but he could see now that a huge drift covered the house. Standing on the show shoes, his chest was as high as the roof's eave, but the snow on the roof was piled higher than his head. Isaac realized that knocking the weight off could be dangerous. If it all came off the steep roof at the same time, it could easily bury him, so he tentatively dug into the overhang, stretching as far as he could with the shovel. A slab dropped off, revealing the wood shingles beneath. Another jab broke free a coffin-sized slab that made a thud he felt through his feet. A crack opened up in the bank of snow that remained on the roof. Isaac backed away as fast as he could as the gap widened, and two thirds of the mass slid ponderously off, leaving only a thin sliver at the ridge.

Snow covered the hole he'd just climbed from, blocking his way back.

"Crackers," he said, the strongest explicative he used. Breath froze on his chin. Before he could get back into the house, though, he needed to sweep the other side. Lifting knees high to clear the snowshoes, he moved around the building.

As he waded through the drift, he thought about the book of Amos, which said, "And I will smite the winter house with the summer house; and the houses of ivory shall perish, and the great houses shall have an end, saith the Lord."

What Isaac needed here was a little smiting.

By the time he'd finished, dug his way back into the generator house and closed the window, he was exhausted, but, more dangerously, he was freezing. The fire in the stove had gone out, and without a buffering layer of snow on the roof, a draft blew through the room. The water wheel had picked up an ominous screech, so instead of trying to light the fire, he put a candle into the Tommie Sticker and walked down the stairs. Ice had formed in the trough where the stream entered the generator wheel, and now water poured onto the floor, deflected by the blockage. The wheel turned half as slow as it should. Water poured onto the floor, some of it freezing against the wood, but most flowing down the slant to the far wall.

Too tired even for a well earned, "Crackers!" he swung the two-pound hammer against the blockage. It barely chipped, and he lost his footing, sprawling beneath the water wheel. Icy water drenched him. Isaac scrambled away, slipping on the slick floor. If he didn't clear the trough soon, the wheel would freeze solid. It could become unusable until spring, and only then after extensive repair.

Carefully, this time, keeping his weight distributed on both feet, he sidled toward the trough, hammer in hand. He thought of Lamech, Noah's father, who the Bible said of, "And he called his name Noah, saying, This same shall comfort us concerning our work and toil of our hands, because of the ground which the LORD hath cursed."

The ice was the curse, the hammer the work. So cold he could hardly hold the heavy tool, Isaac swung it against the obstruction.

When she woke again, an elderly man leaned over the cocoon. "Don't move, Meghan. You shouldn't feel pain, but you're likely to be nauseous for a few minutes."

She closed her eyes. I'm five hundred and twenty years old now, she thought. Over thirty-five hundred years to go.

When she opened her eyes, the old man still leaned in, looking concerned. His hand reached over the edge to cup her upper arm. "Are you okay?"

Tentatively, she nodded, then waited to see if the movement would bother her. Her stomach twisted, but the discomfort passed. "I think so." Her joints didn't ache, but her thinking felt fuzzy. She looked at him closely. "Crew Chief Teague?" He shook his head. "No, he's dead." She squinted. "Dr. Arnold?"

He nodded. "I'm still Sean. It took years to figure out what was wrong with the long sleep."

"How many?"

"Almost forty."

She remembered Sean's smooth skin. How he felt when she woke but he still slept. How he'd held her when she talked about Earth and her fears.

"I'm dying," she had said, their last night together. "We will never get to where we are going, and we will never go back."

The night before, a hundred years earlier, Sean had rocked her gently, holding her head to his chest. "We're not dead yet."

Now, Meghan didn't recognize his eyes. He held out a hand to help her from the cocoon, but she didn't take it. He was a stranger. She sat up on her own, felt sick again. When it passed, and she climbed out, Sean stood back, looking at her sadly. "I missed you," he said.

"It's only been a few minutes for me."

"That's true."

She stood awkwardly for a minute, unsure of what to say.

Finally, she offered, "I have work to do."

"Of course. Me too." Lights flickered on the other cocoons, and she realized he'd woken her first.

For the first week, she only saw him at meals, but she sat on the other side of the cafeteria. She tried not to think about the blank wall and her candle holder keepsake. With effort, she avoided pulling the box from under the bed. She thought, maybe if I don't look at it, I won't long for it. I won't miss it. Meghan concentrated on the hydroponic tanks. Every connection needed to be refitted. She retooled valves, serviced pumps, recalibrated the chemical testing equipment, and met with the horticulturists who talked about genetic drift, mutations and evolution. Over the course of five hundred years, the plants adapted to the artificial environment. The most efficient at extracting nutrients from the fluids flourished. The more aggressive that grew faster or taller crowded out their weaker cousins.

She couldn't sleep during her rest hours, so she wandered back to the hydroponics rooms. All the plants were low growers, flourishing under lights hanging from the ceiling. Tomatoes, strawberries, cucumbers, ferns of various sorts, beets, peppers and numerous others. Nothing that grew tall. Tree seeds were held in storage for planet fall when they reached Zeta Reticula, although there was a question if they would germinate. No one had ever planted a four thousand year-old seed before. She walked down the long row, letting the palm of her hand brush the plant tops while imagining the aspen the ship carried. Would there be an aspen grove one day on the planet orbiting Zeta Reticula? Aspen preferred to spread from their roots. If just one seed germinated, she could grow a forest. Would Earth trees flourish so far from their native sun?

The fear gathered in her chest like a tightness, so she rubbed her fist between her breasts as she walked, trying to work through the tension. At the end of the row of vegetation, she looked up one of the ship's long spokes, a huge hollow chamber that reached the ship's core, the center they revolved around to produce the illusion of gravity. She'd grown used to the effect that had disoriented her at first, moving from the claustrophobic pressure of the growing room to the shocking reach of empty space. She crossed the fifty-foot diameter of the spoke to get to the next row of plants.

At the end of the final work day before entering the cocoon again, she walked through the plants one last time. They smelled wet and vaguely chemical, but not green, not natural at all, so she kept going until she reached Sean's room and raised her hand to knock. She paused. It seemed that only two weeks ago she had kissed a young man goodbye. She couldn't picture the ship without him. Every day she expected to see him turn a corner, to join her in the hydroponic labs. He never did. Instead, an old man looked at her mournfully when she passed by. He sacrificed forty years to save her and the rest. She almost left.

When he opened the door, Meghan said, "I missed you too."

Sean let her in, the age spots on his hand were prominent in the harsh, hallway light. "I have something for you." He opened a drawer and removed the metal candle holder. "I know how much it meant. I thought about having them open it for you. We could find out if there's anything inside."

She traced her finger along the loop where the candle would have been placed. Rubbed the rough brass cap at one end. If held the wrong way, it looked like a weapon, the five-inch long, narrow spike that would hold the antique in a mine wall or stuck into wood could also hurt someone. "I'd forgotten about it," she lied.

As they talked quietly in his room, she started to see the man she used to know. Beneath the thinning hair, behind the wrinkles and tiredness, she recognized him.

When they slipped under the sheets later, Sean said, "I don't have as much to offer as I did before. I'm not . . . young."

"Just hold me, then, and let's sleep."

But after hours of listening to his soft breathing and thinking that he still sounded a little like wind through aspens, he woke up, and Meghan found he had more life in him than he thought.

Isaac stood next to the cold stove. His clothes no longer dripped. They crackled when he moved. Next to his skin, though, they were soaked, and he could feel them sucking away the little heat that remained. One ceiling board had broken completely while he'd knocked the snow off the roof, and the supplies directly underneath were covered, including the boxes of matches. He scooped snow off the floor in double handfuls until he found them, but the boxes were squashed and the matches ruined. The match heads smeared against the striker when he tried to light them.

Dully, his head feeling sluggish and slow, he knelt on the pile of snow for a minute. Flakes came down through the hole in the room, swirling in a breeze that hadn't been there before. Without matches, he'd never light the fire. Maybe he could get the snowshoes back on and make his way to the miners' cabins, but he knew the steep trail, completely hidden in the storm, would be almost impossible to hike, even if his clothes weren't already wet and he wasn't exhausted. He couldn't feel his knees against the snow, and the cold crept up his legs. He thought about just staying still. His chin drifted to his chest. Resting sounded good. In a few minutes, he would get up, but for now, a little sleep was all he needed. The vibration and steady thumping of the generator below annoyed him though, then, frightened, he stood. If he slept, the generator would surely freeze, and so would he. If he didn't have duties, he could rest, but the others depended on him.

Isaac waved his arms to restore circulation, slapping his hands against his arms, then staggered toward the stairs. With renewed vigor, the wind shook the house. No light came from the depths. His candle had gone out, so he swept his hand against the wood, careful to not fall again on the slick floor, until he hit the Tommie Sticker. Water gurgled against the power wheel behind him. With a yank, he pulled the candle holder from the wood, forced himself to climb the stairs, before sitting by the stove. It took a dozen tries to unscrew the brass cap holding the matches. There were only three. Carefully, he lit one, but before he touched the candle, the breeze blew it out. He nearly wept. With the new hole in the roof, there was no place he could guarantee the next match would stay lit long enough to start the fire.

He opened the stove door, pushed his hands inside, out of the wind, to light the second match. It flicked to life, but the draw up the chimney immediately snuffed it out.

Isaac took a deep breath, closed the stove flue to stop the wind, and mumbled a prayer before lighting the last match. The water in his shoes felt like it was freezing. He couldn't feel his feet at all. The match caught, held steady. Carefully, he pushed the candle wick into the flame. It flared into life. He jammed the candle between two charcoaled logs in the stove before feeding kindling to the flame. Soon, smoke flowed from the open stove. Isaac coughed, and his eyes teared, as he kicked the stool apart for bigger pieces of wood, the last fuel in the house, but he didn't open the flue until a healthy flame filled the iron stove. Heat baked off the sides. His gloves steamed on top of the stove as he warmed his hands. Piece by piece, he removed his clothes to hang around the stove before wrapping his blanket around his shivering shoulders. Water dripped from his coat and pants. Heat rolled off the stove, tingling his cheeks, sending stabbing sparks through his toes and feet. He grimaced and moved closer.

The wood walls of the house rattled in a torrent of wind, whipping the fire in the little stove into a tiny inferno. At its peak, when surely the house would have to shatter, the wind stopped, and for the first time in a ten days, the house fell silent except for the river's heart beating through the generator below.

The storm had broken.

In the cabin's sudden quiet, Isaac reached for his bible, opened it randomly to read the first verse his eye fell upon. Surely the storm's cessation was a miracle. Surely a message would be at hand. He wrote the verse on a slip of paper, rolled it into a tube, then sealed it inside the Tommy Sticker. By the time he finished, his face felt warm and his toes stopped aching.

Sean didn't wake up after the seventh long sleep.

Dr. Singh said, "He knew the dangers when he let himself age. The sleep process is hard. I'm sorry." She consulted her notes. "Dr. Arnold was a great man. His work on long sleep cellular degradation and preservation was groundbreaking. If we were still on Earth, he surely would receive a Nobel Prize. We should all make it to Zeta Reticula because of him." Singh shook her head sympathetically. "I understand you were close."

Meghan gripped the edge of the examination table. "I saw him yesterday . . . before the last sleep I mean. I just saw him." She felt every minute of her seven hundred and twenty-two years.

"Me too," said Singh. "If you need them, I can prescribe anti-depressants, but I'd rather not. Drug interaction is difficult to predict."

Meghan walked the long hall from the infirmary to Sean's apartment. The plastic sheets covered his bed and the desk, coated by a thin layer of dust. Despite automated cleaning mechanisms, dust still fell on surfaces they couldn't reach. She pulled the plastic off his desk and let it fall to the floor. He'd left a notebook and her candle holder in the middle. She turned the cover back carefully. The paper that started the trip seven hundred years ago, even though it was acid free and specially milled to last, had become brittle. Any hand-written notes that were expected to be permanent were written on plastic paper, but Sean had enjoyed the feel of real pages better.

He had written "To Meghan" inside the cover; the rest of the pages were blank.

When she sat on the edge of the bed, the plastic crackled. The candle holder rested on her lap. She wondered, did everyone feel so empty, and what could she do about it? Her fingers pressed against the cool metal. Although remembering the aspen shaking in the valley of her wall display escaped her, she felt connected through the hard shape. How often had this candle holder stuck in a mine wall to light a few feet of rock? Who else had held it? Had it ever been more than just a tool to them? Her fingers traveled from the pointed end, past the coil that held the candle, to the burnished brass tube. For the first time, Meghan really examined the antique as a practical object instead of art. Was that a cap on the end of what she had thought was the handle? She twisted it hard. Nothing. Maybe the antique did have something in it, another connection to Earth. Both Teague and Sean had wondered, now she wanted to know.

A few minutes later she asked the machine shop chief, a stout woman whose name Meghan had never known, "Do you have a way to open it?"

The chief turned it over. She said, "It's brass, I think. From the 19th Century, you say? I can cut it apart, but it will cause damage."

"Go ahead."

The chief handled the cutting tool delicately, sending tiny sparks flurrying as she sliced through the candle holder's end. A coin-sized piece of metal dropped to the floor. Meghan leaned over her shoulder as the chief used a pair of tweezers to pull the rolled up slip of paper from the cavity.

Meghan shivered. "It's almost a thousand years old!"

"There's writing."

"A message." Meghan feared the paper would crumble before she could discover what it said.

"What does it mean?" asked the shop chief after they'd carefully unrolled it.

"It's a bible verse, I think. I think I know."

Meghan left the puzzled shop chief behind and headed toward hydroponics, already planning new pipes and grow lights. She would have to leave explanations and instructions for the next shift's hydroponic officers.

Isaac climbed through the window and up to the surface again, the last of the chair burning in the stove behind him. The air bit just as cruelly, but without the wind behind it, and the clouds clearing, he didn't feel as cold, although dampness squished in his temporarily warm clothes. If he couldn't find more wood soon, though, the fire would wink out again, and storm or no storm, he would freeze. Holding a short-handled axe, he girded himself for the long hike up the canyon where he might be able to find firewood.

For a moment, he tried to orient himself. Snow transformed the valley, hiding all that had been familiar. The hundreds of tree trunks that marked the land before were deeply covered so the vista before him was smooth, clean, and hypnotic. The Crystal River had almost entirely vanished, revealed only by a narrow crack in the snow from where the water's glassy voice arose.

What surprised him most, though, were the trees that remained. Two weeks earlier, their lowest branches were twenty feet above the ground, the easy to reach ones having been chopped off for wood. Now, though, where the snow drifted, their needles brushed the crystalline surface. He would have no trouble finding fuel. He thought, why that tree there carries enough dead limbs to keep me warm for a month. It felt like a miracle.

He thought about the Bible verse he'd written on the slip of paper. He wasn't sure what it meant, but it had filled him with hope: "Come, let us take our fill of love until the morning: let us solace ourselves with loves. For the goodman is not at home, he is gone a long journey." A bit from Proverbs.

When spring came, he would take the Tommie Sticker with its message and bury it by the pump house. Somewhere, someone might read it, and it would help. He was sure of it.

Meghan kept her eyes closed for a long time after she awoke until, finally, Dr. Singh's familiar voice said, "I know you can hear me. Your vitals don't lie."

"I'm eight hundred and twenty-two years old today." She hadn't moved even a finger yet, but she didn't feel tired like she had the last time. She only felt hopeful.

She waited through Dr. Singh's tests impatiently. "I have to get to work," Meghan said.

Rushing through the hallways, she barely acknowledged other crew members' greetings. They, too, had work to do. So much of the trip waited before them. So much more space had to be traversed before they could come to a rest.

The first hydroponics lab looked much like she had left it, although she noted the tanks that held the plants steady would need rebuilding on her shift. She passed under one of the spokes, the cathedral-like height earning not a glance. Did her experiment work, she thought. Did the other hydroponics officers follow her direction? She couldn't see far in front of her. The ceiling's downward bulge cut off her view until she was almost there, and then, she saw.

At the end of the row, where normally the plants stopped, her jury-rigged piping led to the new plant tanks. A thick trunk rose from the tank, and as she entered the space below the next spoke, her gaze traveled up the tree's long stretch. Guy wires attached to the vertical space's sides held the tree steady. At the top, new grow fixtures hung suspended from other wires, bathing the aspen in light.

Meghan held her breath. An aspen, under the right conditions, can grow to eighty feet. This one was easily that tall. She walked around the tree. New piping and tanks connected to her original work. Three other trees grew from them. The closest tank came from her co-worker twenty-five years down the line, and the tree from that tank nearly matched her own. A smaller tree, only fifty years old, grew from the next tank, and the last tank held the smallest tree, still over thirty feet to its top. The history attached to it showed it had been built twenty-five years ago. Each officer had added a tree to the grove.

Meghan sat on the floor so she could look up with less strain. Each tree's branches touched the next. The room smelled of aspen, a light leafy odor that reminded her of mountains and streams, and an old generator house perched on the edge of a short cliff.

After she'd sat for a while, she realized that air currents in the ship flowed up the spoke. What she heard, finally, was not the ubiquitous mechanical hiss from the ventilation vents. What she heard was the gentle rustle of leaves touching leaves, a sound that she thought she'd long left behind and would never hear again.

Originally published in *Analog Science Fiction and Fact,* June 2009.

ABOUT THE AUTHOR

James Van Pelt is a writer who also serves as an English teacher in the language arts department at the Fruita Monument High School in Fruita, Colorado. A prolific short-story writer, his stories have been finalists for the Nebula Award and the Theodore Sturgeon Award, and he himself has been a finalist for the John W. Campbell Award for Best New Writer. His stories have been gathered in four collections, *Strangers and Beggars, The Last of the O-Forms and Other Stories, The Radio Magician and Other Stories,* and *Flying in the Heart of the Lafayette Escadrille,* and he has also published a novel, *Summer of the Apocalypse.* Coming up is a new novel, *Pandora's Gun.* Van Pelt lives in Grand Junction, Colorado.

Tyche and the Ants
HANNU RAJANIEMI

The ants arrived on the Moon on the same day Tyche went through the Secret Door to give a ruby to the Magician.

She was glad to be out of the Base. The Brain had given her a Treatment earlier that morning, and that always left her tingly and nervous, with pent-up energy that could only be expended by running down the gray rolling slope down the side of Malapert Mountain, jumping and hooting.

"Come on, keep up!" she shouted at the grag that the Brain had inevitably sent to keep an eye on her. The white-skinned machine followed her on its two thick treads, cylindrical arms swaying for balance as it rumbled laboriously downhill, following the little craters of Tyche's footprints.

Exasperated, she crossed her arms and paused to wait. She looked up. The mouth of the Base was hidden from view, as it should be, to keep them safe from space sharks. The jagged edge of the mountain hid the Great Wrong Place from sight, except for a single wink of blue malice, just above the gleaming white of the upper slopes, a stark contrast against the velvet black of the sky. The white was not snow—that was a Wrong Place thing—but tiny beads of glass made by ancient meteor impacts. That's what the Brain said, anyway. According to Chang'e the Moon Girl, it was all the jewels she had lost over the centuries she had lived here.

Tyche preferred Chang'e's version. That made her think of the ruby, and she touched her belt pouch to make sure it was still there.

"Outings are subject to being escorted at all times," said the sonorous voice of the Brain in her helmet. "There is no reason to be impatient."

Most of the grags were autonomous: the Brain could only control a few of them at a time. But of course it would keep an eye on her, so soon after the Treatment.

"Yes, there is, slowpoke," Tyche muttered, stretching her arms and jumping up and down in frustration.

Her suit flexed and flowed around her with the movement. She had grown it herself as well, the third one so far, although it had taken much longer than the ruby. Its many layers were alive, it felt light, and best of all, it had a powerskin, a slick porous tissue made from cells with mechanosensitive ion channels that translated her movements into power for the suit. It was so much better than the white clumsy fabric ones the Chinese had left behind; the grags had cut and sewn a baby-sized version out of those for her that kind of worked, but was impossibly stuffy and stiff.

It was only the second time she had tested the new suit, and she was proud of it: it was practically a wearable ecosystem, and she was pretty sure that with its photosynthesis layer, it would keep her alive for months, if she only had enough sunlight and carried enough of the horrible compressed Chinese nutrients.

She frowned. Her legs were suddenly gray, mottled with browns. She brushed them with her hand, and her fingers—slick silvery hue of the powerskin—came away the same color. It seemed the regolith dust clung to the suit. Annoying. She absently noted to do something about it for the next iteration when she fed the suit back into the Base's big biofabber.

Now the grag was stuck on the lip of a shallow crater, grinding treads sending up silent parabolas of little rocks and dust. Tyche had had enough of waiting.

"I'll be back for dinner," she told the Brain.

Without waiting for the Base mind's response, she switched off the radio, turned around, and started running.

Tyche settled into the easy stride the Jade Rabbit had shown her: gliding just above the surface, using well-timed toe-pushes to cross craters and small rocks that littered the uneven regolith.

She took the long way around, avoiding her old tracks that ran down much of the slope, just to confuse the poor grag more. She skirted around the edge of one of the pitch-black cold fingers—deeper craters that never got sunlight—that were everywhere on this side of the mountain. It would have been a shortcut, but it was too cold for her suit. Besides, the ink-men lived in the deep potholes, in the Other Moon beyond the Door.

Halfway around, the ground suddenly shook. Tyche slid uncontrollably, almost going over the edge before she managed to stop by turning around mid-leap and jamming her toes into the chilly hard regolith when she landed. Her heart pounded. Had the ink-men brought something up from the deep dark, something big? Or had she just been almost hit by a meteorite? That had happened a couple of times, a sudden crater blooming soundlessly into being, right next to her.

Then she saw beams of light in the blackness and realized that it was only the Base's sandworm, a giant articulated machine with a maw full of toothy wheels that ground Helium-3 and other volatiles from the deep shadowy deposits.

Tyche breathed a sigh of relief and continued on her way. Many of the grag bodies were ugly, but she liked the sandworm. She had helped to program it: constantly toiling, it went into such deep places that the Brain could not control it remotely.

The Secret Door was in a shallow crater, maybe a hundred meters in diameter. She went down its slope with little choppy leaps and stopped her momentum with a deft pirouette and toe-brake, right in front of the Door.

It was made of two large pyramid-shaped rocks, leaning against each other at a funny angle, with a small triangular gap between them: the Big Old One, and the Troll. The Old One had two eyes made from shadows, and when Tyche squinted from the right angle, a rough outcrop and a groove in the base became a nose and a mouth. The Troll looked grumpy, half-squashed against the bigger rock's bulk.

As she watched, the face of the Old One became alive and gave her a quizzical look. Tyche gave it a stiff bow—out of habit, even though she could have curtsied in her new suit.

How have you been, Tyche? the rock asked, in its silent voice.

"I had a Treatment today," she said dourly.

The rock could not nod, so it raised its eyebrows.

Ah. Always Treatments. Let me tell you, in my day, vacuum was the only treatment we had, and the sun, and a little meteorite every now and then to keep clean. Stick to that and you'll live to be as old as I am.

And as fat, grumbled the Troll. Believe me, once you carry him for a few million years, you start to feel it. What are you doing here, anyway?

Tyche grinned. "I made a ruby for the Magician." She took it out and held it up proudly. She squeezed it a bit, careful not to damage her suit's gloves against the rough edges, and held it in the Old One's jet-black shadow, knocking it against the rock's surface. It sparkled with tiny embers, just like it was supposed to. She had made it herself, using Verneuil flame fusion, and spiced it with a piezoelectric material so that it would convert motion to light.

It's very beautiful, Tyche, the Old One said. I'm sure he will love it.

Oh? said the troll. Well, maybe the old fool will finally stop looking for the Queen Ruby, then, and settle down with poor Chang'e. In with you, now. You're encouraging this sentimental piece of rubble here. He might start crying. Besides, everybody is waiting.

Tyche closed her eyes, counted to ten, and crawled through the opening between the rocks, through the Secret Door to her Other Moon.

The moment Tyche opened her eyes she saw that something was wrong. The house of the Jade Rabbit was broken. The boulders she had carefully balanced on top of each other lay scattered on the ground, and the lines she had drawn to make the rooms and the furniture were smudged. (Since it never rained, the house had not needed a roof.)

There was a silent sob. Chang'e the Moon Girl sat next to the Rabbit's house, crying. Her flowing silk robes of purple, yellow, and red were a mess on the ground like broken wings, and her makeup had been running down her pale, powdered face.

"Oh, Tyche!" she cried. "It is terrible, terrible!" She wiped a crystal tear from her eye. It evaporated in the vacuum before it could fall on the dust. Chang'e was a drama queen, and pretty, and knew it, too. Once, she had an affair with the Woodcutter just because she was bored, and bore him children, but they were already grown up and had moved to the Dark Side.

Tyche put her hands on her hips, suddenly angry. "Who did this?" she asked. "Was it the Cheese Goat?"

Tearful, Chang'e shook her head.

"General Nutsy Nutsy? Or Mr. Cute?" The Moon People had many enemies, and there had been times when Tyche had led them in great battles, cutting her way through armies of stone with an aluminum rod the Magician had enchanted into a terrible bright blade. But none of them had ever been so mean as to smash the houses.

"Who was it, then?"

Chang'e hid her face behind one flowing silken sleeve and pointed. And that's when Tyche saw the first ant, moving in the ruins of the Jade Rabbit's house.

It was not like a grag or an otho, and certainly not a Moon Person. It was a jumbled metal frame, all angles and shiny rods, like a vector calculation come to life, too straight and rigid against the rough surfaces of the rocks to be real. It was like two tetrahedrons inside each other, with a bulbous sphere at each vertex, each glittering like the eye of the Great Wrong Place.

It was not big, perhaps reaching up to Tyche's knees. One of the telescoping metal struts had white letters on it. ANT-A3972, they said, even though the thing did not look like the ants Tyche had seen in videos.

It stretched and moved like the geometrical figures Tyche manipulated with a gesture during the Brain's math lessons. Suddenly, it flipped over the Rabbit's broken wall, making Tyche gasp. Then it shifted into a strange, slug-like motion over the regolith, first stretching, then contracting. It made Tyche's skin crawl. As she watched, the ant thing fell into a crevice between two boulders—but dexterously pulled itself up, supported itself on a couple of vertices, and somersaulted over the obstacle like an acrobat.

Tyche stared at it. Anger started to build up in her chest. In the Base, she obeyed the Brain and the othos and the grags because she had Promised. But the Other Moon was her place: it belonged to her and the Moon People, and no one else.

"Everybody else is hiding," whispered Chang'e. "You have to do something, Tyche. Chase it away."

"Where is the Magician?" Tyche asked. *He would know what to do.* She did not like the way the ant thing moved.

As she hesitated, the creature swung around and, with a series of twitches, pulled itself up into a pyramid, as if watching her. *It's not so nasty-looking,* Tyche thought. *Maybe I could bring it back to the Base, introduce it to Hugbear.* It would be a complex operation: she would have to assure the bear that she would always love it no matter what, and then carefully introduce the newcomer to it—

The ant thing darted forward, and a sharp pain stung Tyche's thigh. One of the thing's vertices had a spike that quickly retracted. Tyche's suit grumbled as it sealed all its twenty-one layers, and soothed the tiny wound. Tears came to her eyes, and her mouth was suddenly dry. No Moon Person had ever hurt her, not even the ink-men, except to pretend. She almost switched her radio on and called the grag for help.

Then she felt the eyes of the Moon People, looking at her from their windows. She gritted her teeth and ignored the bite of the wound. She was Tyche. She was brave. Had she not climbed to the Peak of Eternal Light once, all alone, following the solar panel cables, just to look the Great Wrong Place in the eye? (It had been smaller than she'd expected, tiny and blue and unblinking, with a bit of white and green, and altogether a disappointment.)

Carefully, Tyche picked up a good-sized rock from the Jade Rabbit's wall—it was broken anyway. She took a slow step towards the creature.

It had suddenly contracted into something resembling a cube and seemed to be absorbed in something. Tyche moved right. The ant flinched at her shadow. She moved left—and swung the rock down as hard as she could.

She missed. The momentum took her down. Her knees hit the hard chilly regolith. The rock bounced away. This time the tears came, but Tyche struggled up and threw the rock after the creature. It was scrambling away, up the slope of the crater.

Tyche picked up the rock and followed. In spite of the steep climb, she gained on it with a few determined leaps, cheered on by the Moon People below. She was right at its heels when it climbed over the edge of the crater. But when she caught a glimpse of what lay beyond, she froze and dropped down on her belly.

A bright patch of sunlight shone on the wide highland plain ahead. It was crawling with ants, hundreds of them. A rectangular carpet of them sat right in the middle, all joined together into a thick metal sheet. Every now and then it undulated like something soft, a shiny amoeba. Other ant things moved in orderly rows, sweeping the surroundings.

The one Tyche was following picked up speed on the level ground, rolling and bouncing, like a skeletal football, and as she watched from her hiding place, it joined the central mass. Immediately, the ant-sheet changed. Its sides stretched upwards into a hollow, cup-like shape: other ants at its base telescoped into a high, supporting structure, lifting it up. A sharp spike grew in the middle of the cup, and then the whole structure turned to point at the sky. *A transmitter,* Tyche thought, following it with her gaze.

It was aimed straight at the Great Wrong Place.

Tyche swallowed, turned around and slid back down. She was almost glad to see the grag down there, waiting for her patiently by the Secret Door.

The Brain did not sound angry, but then the Brain was never angry.

"Evacuation procedure has been initiated," it said. "This location has been compromised."

Tyche was breathing hard: the Base was in a lava tube halfway up the south slope of the mountain, and the way up was always harder than the way down. This time, the grag had had no trouble keeping up with her. It had been a silent journey: she had tried to tell the Brain about the ants, but the AI had maintained complete radio silence until they were inside the Base.

"What do you mean, *evacuation*?" Tyche demanded.

She opened the helmet of her suit and breathed in the comfortable yeasty smell of her home module. Her little home was converted from one of the old Chinese ones, snug white cylinders that huddled close to the main entrance of the cavernous lava tube. She always thought they looked like the front teeth in the mouth of a big snake.

The main tube itself was partially pressurized, over sixty meters in diameter and burrowed deep into the mountain. It split into many branches, expanded and reinforced by othos and grags with regolith concrete pillars. She had tried to play it there many times, but preferred the Other Moon: she did not like the stench from the bacteria that the othos seeded the walls with, the ones that pooped calcium and aluminum.

Now, it was a hotbed of activity. The grags had set up bright lights and moved around, disassembling equipment and filling cryogenic tanks. The walls were alive with the tiny, soft, starfish-like othos, eating bacteria away. The Brain had not wasted any time.

"We are leaving, Tyche," the Brain said. "You need to get ready. The probe you found knows we are here. We are going away, to another place. A safer place. Do not worry. We have alternative locations prepared. It will be fine."

Tyche bit her lip. *It's my fault.* She wished the Brain had a proper face. It had a module of its own, in the coldest, unpressurized part of the tube, where its quantum processors could operate undisturbed, but inside it was just lasers and lenses and trapped ions, and rat brain cells grown to mesh with circuitry. How could it understand about the Jade Rabbit's house? It wasn't fair.

"And before we go, you need a Treatment."

Going away. She tried to wrap her mind around the concept. They had always been here, to be safe from the space sharks from the Great Wrong Place. And the Secret Door was here. If they went somewhere else, how would she find her way to the Other Moon? What would the Moon People do without her?

And she still hadn't given the ruby to the Magician.

The anger and fatigue exploded out of her in one hot wet burst.

"I'm not going to go not going to go not going to go," she said and ran into her sleeping cubicle. "And I don't want a stupid Treatment," she yelled, letting the door membrane congeal shut behind her.

Tyche took off her suit, flung it into a corner and cuddled against the Hugbear in her bed. Its ragged fur felt warm against her cheek, and its fake heartbeat was reassuring. She distantly remembered her Mum had made it move from afar, sometimes, stroked her hair with its paws, its round facescreen replaced with her features. That had been a long time ago and she was sure the bear was bigger then. But it was still soft.

Suddenly, the bear moved. Her heart jumped with a strange, aching hope. But it was only the Brain. "Go 'way," she muttered.

"Tyche, this is important," said the Brain. "Do you remember what you promised?"

She shook her head. Her eyes were hot and wet. *I'm not going to cry like Chang'e,* she thought. *I'm not.*

"Do you remember now?"

The bear's face was replaced with a man and a woman. The man had no hair and his dark skin glistened. The woman was raven-haired and pale, with a face like a bird. *Mum is even prettier than Chang'e,* Tyche thought.

"Hello, Tyche," they said in unison, and laughed. "We are Kareem and Sofia," the woman said. "We are your mommy and daddy. We hope you are well when you see this." She touched the screen, quickly and lightly, like a little bunny hop on the regolith.

"But if the Brain is showing you this," Tyche's Dad said, "then it means that something bad has happened and you need to do what the Brain tells you."

"You should not be angry at the Brain," Mum said. "It is not like we are, it just plans and thinks. It just does what it was told to do. And we told it to keep you safe."

"You see, in the Great Wrong Place, people like us could not be safe," Dad continued. "People like Mum and me and you were feared. They called us Greys, after the man who figured out how to make us, and they were jealous, because we lived longer than they did and had more time to figure things out. And because giving things silly names makes people feel better about themselves. Do we look gray to you?"

No. Tyche shook her head. The Magician was gray, but that was because he was always looking for rubies in dark places and never saw the sun.

"So we came here, to build a Right Place, just the two of us." Her Dad squeezed Mum's shoulders, just like the bear used to do to Tyche. "And you were born here. You can't imagine how happy we were."

Then Mum looked serious. "But we knew that the Wrong Place people might come looking for us. So we had to hide you, to make sure you would be safe, so they would not look inside you and cut you and find out what makes you work. They would do anything to have you."

Fear crunched Tyche's gut into a tiny cold ball. *Cut you?*

"It was very, very hard, dear Tyche, because we love you. Very hard, not to touch you except from afar. But we want you to grow big and strong, and when the time comes, we will come and find you, and then we will all be in the Right Place together."

"But you have to promise to take your Treatments. Can you promise to do that? Can you promise to do what the Brain says?"

"I promise," Tyche muttered.

"Goodbye, Tyche," her parents said. "We will see you soon."

And then they were gone, and the Hugbear's face was blank and pale brown again.

"We need to go soon," the Brain said again, and this time its voice sounded more gentle. "Please get ready. I would like you to have a Treatment before travel."

Tyche sighed and nodded. It wasn't fair. But she had promised.

The Brain sent Tyche a list of things she could take with her, scrolling in one of the windows of her room. It was a short list. She looked around at the fabbed figurines and the moon rock that she thought looked like a boy and the e-sheets floating everywhere with her favorite stories open. She could not even take the Hugbear. She felt alone, suddenly, like she had when she climbed to look at the Great Wrong Place on top of the mountain.

Then she noticed the ruby lying on her bed. *If I go away and take it with me, the Magician will never find it.* She thought about the Magician and his panther, desperately looking from crater to crater, forever. *It's not fair. Even if I keep my promise, I'll have to take it to him.*

And say goodbye.

Tyche sat down on the bed and thought very hard.

The Brain was everywhere, but it could not watch everything. It was based on a scanned human brain, some poor person who had died a long time ago. It had no cameras in her room. And its attention would be on the evacuation: it would have to keep programming and reprogramming the grags. She picked at the sensor bracelet in her wrist that monitored her life signs and location. That was the difficult bit. She would have to do something about that. But there wasn't much time: the Brain would take her for a Treatment soon.

She hugged the bear again in frustration. It felt warm, and as she squeezed it hard, she could feel its pulse—

Tyche sat up. She remembered the Jade Rabbit's stories and tricks, the tar rabbit he had made to trick an enemy.

She reached into the Hugbear's head and pulled out a programming window, coupled it with her sensor. She summoned up old data logs, added some noise to them. Then she fed them to the bear, watched its pulse and breathing and other simulated life signs change to match hers.

Then she took a deep breath, and as quickly as she could, she pulled off the bracelet and put it on the Hugbear.

"Tyche? Is there something wrong?" the Brain asked.

Tyche's heart jumped. Her mind raced. "It's fine," she said. "I think . . . I think I just banged my sensor a bit. I'm just getting ready now." She tried to make her voice sound sweet, like a girl who always keeps her promises.

"Your Treatment will be ready soon," the Brain said and was gone. Heart pounding, Tyche started to put on her suit.

There was a game that Tyche used to play in the lava tube: how far could she get before she was spotted by the grags? She played it now, staying low, avoiding their camera eyes, hiding behind rock protrusions, crates, and cryogenic tanks, until she was in a tube branch that only had othos in it. The Brain did not usually control them directly, and besides, they did not have eyes. Still, her heart felt like meteorite impacts in her chest.

She pushed through a semi-pressurizing membrane. In this branch, the othos had dug too deep for calcium, and caused a roof collapse. In the dim green light of her suit's fluorescence, she made way her up the tube's slope. *There.* She climbed on a pile of rubble carefully. The othos had once told her there was an opening there, and she hoped it would be big enough for her to squeeze through.

Boulders rolled under her, and she felt a sharp bang against her knee. The suit hissed at the sudden impact. She ignored the pain and ran her fingers along the rocks, following a very faint air current she could not have sensed without the suit. Then her fingers met regolith instead of rock. It was packed tight, and she had to push hard at it with her aluminum rod before it gave away. A shower of dust and rubble fell on her, and for a moment she thought there was going to be another collapse. But then there was a patch of velvet sky in front of her. She widened the opening, made herself as small as she could and crawled towards it.

Tyche emerged onto the mountainside. The sudden wide open space of rolling gray and brown around her felt like the time she had eaten too much sugar. Her legs and hands were wobbly, and she had to sit down for a moment. She shook herself: she had an appointment to keep. She checked that the ruby was still in its pouch, got up, and started downwards with the Rabbit's lope.

• • •

The Secret Door was just the way Tyche had left it. She eyed the crater edge nervously, but there were no ants in sight. She bit her lip when she looked at the Old One and the Troll.

What's wrong? the Old One asked.

"I'm going to have to go away."

Don't worry. We'll still be here when you come back.

"I might never come back," Tyche said, choking a bit.

Never is a very long time, the Old One said. Even I have never seen never. We'll be here. Take care, Tyche.

Tyche crawled through to the Other Moon, and found the Magician waiting for her.

He was very thin and tall, taller than the Old One even, and cast a long cold finger of a shadow in the crater. He had a sad face and a scraggly beard and white gloves and a tall top hat. Next to him lay his flying panther, all black, with eyes like tiny rubies.

"Hello, Tyche," the Magician said, with a voice like the rumble of the sandworm.

Tyche swallowed and took out the ruby from her pouch, holding it out to him.

"I made this for you." *What if he doesn't like it?* But the Magician picked it up, slowly, eyes glowing, held it in both hands and gazed at it in awe.

"That is very, very kind of you," he whispered. Very carefully, he took off his hat and put the ruby in it. It was the first time Tyche had ever seen the Magician smile. Still, there was a sadness to his expression.

"I didn't want to leave before giving it to you," she said.

"That's quite a fuss you caused for the Brain. He is going to be very worried."

"He deserves it. But I promised I would go with him."

The Magician looked at the ruby one more time and put the hat back on his head.

"Normally, I don't interfere with the affairs of other people, but for this, I owe you a wish."

Tyche took a deep breath. "I don't want to live with the grags and the othos and the Brain anymore. I want to be in the Right Place with Mum and Dad."

The Magician looked at her sadly.

"I'm sorry, Tyche, but I can't make that happen. My magic is not powerful enough."

"But they promised—"

"Tyche, I know you don't remember. And that's why we Moon People remember for you. The space sharks came and took your parents, a long time ago. They are dead. I am sorry."

Tyche closed her eyes. *A picture in a window, a domed crater. Two bright things arcing over the horizon, like sharks. Then, brightness—*

"You've lived with the Brain ever since. You don't remember because it makes you forget with the Treatments, so you don't get too sad, so you stay the way your parents wanted to keep you. But we remember. And we always tell you the truth."

And suddenly they were all there, all the Moon People, coming from their houses: Chang'e and her children and the Jade Rabbit and the Woodcutter, looking at her gravely and nodding their heads.

Tyche could not bear to look at them. She covered her helmet with her hands, turned around, crawled through the Secret Door and ran away, away from the Other Moon. She ran, not a Rabbit run but a clumsy jerky crying run, until she stumbled on a boulder and went rolling higgledy-piggledy down. She lay curled up in the chilly regolith for a long time. And when she opened her eyes, the ants were all around her.

The ants were arranged around her in a half-circle, stretched into spiky pyramids, waving slightly, as if looking for something. Then they spoke. At first, it was just noise, hissing in her helmet, but after a second it resolved into a voice.

"—hello," it said, warm and female, like Chang'e, but older and deeper. "I am Alissa. Are you hurt?"

Tyche was frozen. She had never spoken to anyone who was not the Brain or one of the Moon People. Her tongue felt stiff.

"Just tell me if you are all right. No one is going to hurt you. Do you feel bad anywhere?"

"No," Tyche breathed.

"There is no need to be afraid. We will take you home." A video feed flashed up inside her helmet, a spaceship that was made up of a cluster of legs and a globe that glinted golden. A circle appeared elsewhere in her field of vision, indicating a tiny pinpoint of light in the sky. "See? We are on our way."

"I don't want to go to the Great Wrong Place," she gasped. "I don't want you to cut me up."

There was a pause.

"Why would we do that? There is nothing to be afraid of."

"Because Wrong Place people don't like people like me."

Another pause.

"Dear child, I don't know what you have been told, but things have changed. Your parents left Earth more than a century ago. We never thought we would find you, but we kept looking. And I'm glad we did. You have been alone on the Moon for a very long time."

Tyche got up, slowly. *I haven't been alone.* Her head spun. *They would do anything to have you.*

She backed off a few steps.

"If I come with you," she asked in a small voice, "will I see Kareem and Sofia again?"

A pause again, longer this time.

"Of course you will," Alissa the ant-woman said finally. "They are right here, waiting for you."

Liar.

Slowly, Tyche started backing off. The ants moved, closing their circle. *I am faster than they are,* she thought. *They can't catch me.*

"Where are you going?"

Tyche switched off her radio, cleared the circle of the ants with a leap and hit the ground running.

Tyche ran, faster than she had ever run before, faster even than when the Jade Rabbit challenged her to a race across the Shackleton Crater. Finally, her lungs and legs burned and she had to stop. She had set out without direction, but had gone up the mountain slope, close to the cold fingers. *I don't want to go back to the Base. The Brain never tells the truth either.* Black dots danced in her eyes. *They'll never catch me.*

She looked back, down towards the crater of the Secret Door. The ants were moving. They gathered into the metal sheet again. Then its sides stretched upwards until they met and formed a tubular structure. It elongated and weaved back and forth and slithered forward, faster than even Tyche could run; a metal snake. The pyramid shapes of the ants glinted in its head like teeth. Faster and faster it came, flowing over boulders and craters like it was weightless, a curtain of billowing dust behind it. She looked around for a hiding place, but she was on open ground now, except for the dark pool of the mining crater to the west.

Then she remembered something the Jade Rabbit had once said. *For anything that wants to eat you, there is something bigger that wants to eat it.*

The ant-snake was barely a hundred meters behind her now, flipping back and forth in sinusoid waves on the regolith like a shiny metal whip. She stuck out her tongue at it, accidentally tasting the sweet inner surface of her helmet. Then she made it to the sunless crater's edge.

With a few bounds, she was over the crater lip. It was like diving into icy water. Her suit groaned, and she could feel its joints stiffening up. But she kept going, towards the bottom, almost blind from the contrast between the pitch-black and the bright sun above. She followed the vibration in her soles. Boulders and pebbles rained on her helmet and she knew the ant-snake was right at her heels.

The lights of the sandworm almost blinded her. *Now.* She leaped up, as high as she could, feeling weightless, reached out for the utility ladder that she knew was on the huge machine's topside. She grabbed it, banged painfully against the worm's side, felt its thunder beneath her.

And then, a grinding, shuddering vibration as the mining machine bit into the ant-snake, rolling right over it.

Metal fragments flew into the air, glowing red-hot. One of them landed on Tyche's arm. The suit made a bubble around it and spat it out. The sandworm came to an emergency halt, and Tyche almost fell off. It started disgorging its little repair grags, and Tyche felt a stab of guilt. She sat still until her breathing calmed down and the suit's complaints about the cold got too loud.

Then she dropped to the ground and started the climb back up, towards the Secret Door.

There were still a few ants left around the Secret Door, but Tyche ignored them. They were rolling around aimlessly, and there weren't enough of them to build a transmitter. She looked up. The ship from the Great Wrong Place was still a distant star. She still had time.

Painfully, bruised limbs aching, she crawled through the Secret Door for one last time.

The Moon People were still there, waiting for her. Tyche looked at them in the eye, one by one. Then she put her hands on her hips.

"I have a wish," she said. "I am going to go away. I'm going to make the Brain obey me, this time. I'm going to go and build a Right Place, all on my own. I'm never going to forget again. So I want you all to come with me." She looked up at the Magician. "Can you do that?"

Smiling, the man in the top hat nodded, spread his white-gloved fingers and whirled his cloak that had a bright red inner lining, like a ruby—

Tyche blinked. The Other Moon was gone. She looked around. She was standing on the other side of the Old One and the Troll, except that they looked just like rocks now. And the Moon People were inside her. *I should feel heavier, carrying so many people,* she thought. But instead she was empty and light.

Uncertainly at first, then with more confidence, she started walking back up Malapert Mountain, towards the Base. Her step was not a rabbit's, nor a panther's, nor a maiden's silky tiptoe, just her very own.

Originally published in *Edge of Infinity*, edited by Jonathan Strahan, 2012.

ABOUT THE AUTHOR

Hannu Rajaniemi was born in Ylivieska, Finland, but spent many years in Edinburgh, Scotland where he received a Ph.D. in string theory, and currently lives in Oakland, California. He is the co☐founder of ThinkTank Maths, which provides consultation service and research in applied mathematics and business development. Rajaniemi has had a big impact on the field with only a relatively small body of work. His first novel, *The Quantum Thief*, was published in 2010 to a great deal of critical buzz and response, and has been followed by two sequels, *The Fractal Prince* and *The Causal Angel*. His most recent book is a collection, *Hannu Rajaniemi: Collected Stories*. Coming up is a new novel, *Summerland*.

Destination: Mars
ANDREW LIPTAK

In recent years, Mars has been back in the news. The wildly successful and dramatic landing of the MINI Cooper-sized rover Curiosity in 2012 has brought a renewed interest in the red planet. In his 2015 State of the Union speech, President Barack Obama reaffirmed NASA's goal to put an astronaut on Mars at some point in the future and organizations such as the Mars One Foundation and SpaceX have set their sights firmly on Martian mission programs.

Mars has always been a likely destination for humanity, and in particular, it has captivated science fiction audiences as a new home, port of call, or simply just a new place to explore. Science fiction's own history of the place has largely evolved alongside that of our own understanding of the planet. As much as we've learned from pictures, probes, and rovers on Mars, the world still has a particular fascination for science fiction authors who have told stories about it up to the present day.

From early in Mars' history, a dichotomy has existed between the urge to study and observe the planet, but also to create and tell stories about it. The Romans named the blood-red point in the sky after their god of war. At the same time, numerous ancient astronomers located in Egypt, Babylon, Greece and others, observed the motion of Mars, and recognized early on that it was different from the other points in the sky: it was a planet, not a star.

Fast forward to the industrial revolution. New scientific principles defined the movements of objects in the solar system, which helped scientists to focus extensively on study of the planets with the aid of new telescopes. Accordingly, authors who had begun to write scientific tales also begun to turn their attention to our nearest neighbors in the solar system. *Brave New Worlds: The Oxford Dictionary of Science Fiction* identifies the first use of the word Martian in 1874, in an American magazine called *The Galaxy*: "The Martians would therefore be in a better position to understand our attempts at opening up a communication than the Venerians."

First Contact

In 1877, Giovanni Schiaparelli created the first detailed map of Mars using a telescope. From his observations, he detailed channels, continents, and seas, terminology rooted in Earth's own geology. In particular, his description of *canali* (channels) was widely mistranslated as canals in English, sparking a wide-spread belief that Mars was home to someone who built them. The description planted the seeds to an idea: Mars was another world like ours, one that could potentially harbor intelligent life.

Percival Lowell followed Schiaparelli's lead in 1894 by constructing an observatory in Arizona, and later publishing a book titled *Mars* in 1895. The book covered his observations of the planet, all the while he speculated on the nature of how beings might live on the planet, drawing from the belief that canals were indeed present on the planet's surface.

In 1897, H.G. Wells published what is possibly the best-known work of science fiction involving Mars: *The War of the Worlds*. From the very beginning of his book, Wells mixes the scientific knowledge of the day into his story: "The planet Mars, I scarcely need remind the reader, revolves about the sun at a mean distance of one hundred forty million miles, and the light and heat it receives from the sun is barely half of that received by this world," all the while constructing a relevant, political story of the day.

The following year, a pair of Edisonade novels: *The Fighters from Mars* (a re-written version of *The War of the Worlds*), and Garrett P. Serviss', *Edison's Conquest of Mars,* was a direct sequel which followed a counterattack on Mars led by Thomas Edison. By basing his aliens on Mars, Wells' *The War of the Worlds* and the various inspired books helped to instill a renewed sense of the historical association of the planet with that of war and destruction.

Romantic Mars

This only continued into the new century, most notably with Edgar Rice Burroughs and some of his best-known works: the Barsoom series featuring Civil War veteran John Carter. Beginning in 1912 with *A Princess of Mars,* Burroughs transports Carter to an inhabited and wild Mars, populating the planet with a rich and complicated civilization for his pulp adventures. His stories inspired numerous others in a burgeoning planetary romance genre: authors ranging from C.S. Lewis with his Space Trilogy, C.L. Moore's Northwest Smith adventures, and Stanley G. Weinbaum with "A Martian Odyssey."

In pulp magazines throughout the early twentieth century, science fiction emerged as its own world and authors began to look beyond Earth for inspiration. Certainly, the idea of a red world would have appealed to the likes of Burroughs, who had spent some time as a cavalry scout in the United States Army before turning to writing. Astronomers had already discerned features from Mars' surface and several authors latched on to the image of the wild west when looking to our nearer planetary neighbors. In "Shambleau," C.L. Moore transported the reader to a dusty and lawless locale that served her stories and characters well.

As late as the 1930s, scientists and astronomers had speculated about the possibility of vegetation on the planet: "*The [American Interplanetary Society] Bulletin* carried an article in January 1932 suggesting the possibility of 'luxuriant vegetation' on Mars along what may or may not have been Lowell's canals."

By the end of the 1940s, Ray Bradbury had taken up the mantle of the planetary romances, with what would later become his own collective work, *The Martian Chronicles* (1950), heavily influenced by the works of Burroughs and other pulp authors. Bradbury's work stood as the last vanguard of a romantic Mars: Bradbury's vividly imagined Mars has helped place it as one of the best works of his generation.

The romantic Mars was a place where we knew people could walk, if not live. While the moon was closer (and certainly had its own share of science fiction stories), Mars held possibility, shrouded in mysteries. Did it have an atmosphere? Was there life? It was a place that sparked our collective imaginations and called to us as a place to go.

And, go we did. In November of 1964, the United States launched a pair of rockets towards Mars. They were the culmination in a larger battle for the planets between the Soviet Union and the United States.

Following the end of the Second World War, each began to develop greater long-ranged weapons to deploy their respective nuclear arsenals. The resulting Space Race followed, which began massive manned spaceflight programs in each country. The United States and Soviet

Union looked first to our Moon as a destination, but many in the space program believed that once we reached the lunar surface, Mars would be our next destination.

Less visible was the race for scientific supremacy, and accordingly, each looked to our two closest neighbors in space: Venus and Mars. Venus, the closer of the two, became the first such battleground, and was closely followed by Mars. Between October 1960 and November 1962, the Soviet Union launched five satellites to Mars: none were successful due to a variety of system or launch failures. The United States didn't fare any better at first either: their first mission, Mariner 3, failed to shed a protective cover, and lost power. Mariner 4, however, successfully reached Mars on July 14th, and would become humanity's first glimpse to the world that we had dreamt so much about.

This first introduction, according to William Burrows in *This New Ocean: The Story of the First Space Age,* " . . . was terrible. Mars was no longer an elusive orange blur with whitish poles and alluring dark blotches. It had been transformed from a place that had recognizable features with which earthlings could identify. Gone were the canals or anything else that could have been purposely dug or built. Gone were the oases holding precious supplies of water. Gone were creatures of any form. Gone, too, were ocean basins, vegetation, or any landscape that even remotely looked like Earth." (Burrows, 464)

The romantic and exotic images of Mars that had been written about from Wells to Burroughs to Moore to Bradbury had been completely shattered. The grainy images transmitted back to Earth showed an alien world—alien even to science fiction authors. Mars was cold, uninhabitable, and dead. While many might have doubted that Mars would have been home to alien life, it was a stark reminder that our science fiction stories sometimes fall short of reality.

Cold Mars

While science fiction's collective vision for what Mars didn't match the real nature of Mars, it did learn and begin to change.

New unmanned missions to Mars followed in the next launch window in 1969. The United States launched Mariner 6 and 7 in February and March, while the USSR missions 2M No.521 in March and 2M No.522 in April failed. 1971 brought new missions: Mariner 8 and Kosmos 419 both failed, but Mariner 9, which launched on May 30th, successfully became the first spacecraft to orbit Mars, where it would spend the next five hundred sixteen days, taking pictures of the planet below. As this happened, humans landed on the Moon for the first time. We were slowly beginning to step into the solar system.

As Mariner 9 approached Mars, NASA's Jet Propulsion Laboratory held a conference with several notable figures: Arthur C. Clarke, Ray Bradbury, Carl Sagan, and others. There, the science fiction authors paid tribute to Stanley G. Weinbaum, Edgar Rice Burroughs, and H.G. Wells for their works in bringing Mars to the imaginations of millions of readers. However, what had become clear was that Mars was not the world so richly imagined; it was a cold, dead world that was difficult to reach. There, Clarke made a bold prediction: "Whether or not there is life on Mars now, there will be by the end of the century." It was a bold claim for a country that would soon be shuttering its manned lunar program, and he would eventually step his estimate ahead several decades. His remarks are important, however, because they positioned how we would tell stories about Mars: no longer a world of exotic life and mystery, it would become the home for a colony, a way point on the way to other planets, a distant outpost.

1976 brought us our next best look at Mars. At the next available window, NASA launched Viking 1 and Viking 2 on August 20th and September 9th, a pair of complicated missions that would, for the first time, land equipment on the surface of Mars. The pair of landers arrived on the surface of the planet on June 19th and August 7th, respectively, and served as humanity's first ambassadors. Their scientific missions included biological and chemical experiments, yielding new insights into the red planet.

The results of the Viking missions provided planetary scientists with a wealth of information, and caught the interest of new science fiction authors. Kim Stanley Robinson noted that he had been particularly inspired by the images sent back by the Viking probes, and felt a yearning to hike and explore the planet's mountain ranges. Over the next decade, he thought about how to terraform the planet, and in 1990, he published the first installment of his Mars trilogy: *Red Mars,* and followed with *Green Mars* and *Blue Mars,* examining a wide range of topics from the planetary science that was being uncovered to the ethical considerations of terraforming a world like Mars. Over the course of the 1990s, other hard science novels about exploring the surface of Mars came out, such as Ben Bova's *Mars* and its sequels.

The planetary romance of the early twentieth century had gone, but in its place were new opportunities for science fiction authors. The research conducted on the surface of Mars opened up the possibilities of new stories of exploration and the scientists and adventurers who boldly went further into the solar system, armed with a new level of realism.

New Missions, New Stories

Our understanding of Mars has only continued to improve. In 1996, the Pathfinder mission with its Sojourner rover became the first such probe on the surface of the planet, exploring its immediate surroundings. Others followed: the Mars Odyssey and Mars Explorer continue to operate on the surface, while another pair of rovers, Spirit and Opportunity, landed in 2003, where each outperformed their designated mission. Spirit shut down in 2010, but Opportunity continues to function, as of the time of this writing. Each mission uncovered, and continues to contribute to our knowledge of Mars. Most recently, millions around the world watched Curiosity touch down in a daring landing in August 2012 that might have come from a science fiction author. Appropriately, Curiosity's landing site was formally named Bradbury Landing. It continues to send back new images every day, and the data it has collected will continue to entrance scientists and science fiction authors for years to come.

The latest string of novels that have taken place on Mars incorporate the latest research from the planet. Andy Weir's breakthrough novel *The Martian* is one such example. Following an astronaut stranded on the planet, Weir drew from books such as *Robinson Crusoe* and scientific work to figure out the central storyline: how would such an astronaut survive?

"All you have to do is start examining any aspect of his survival and you'll quickly find the problems he runs into. He's going to need food, but you can't just create food that easily; you need to actually grow it. Doing some math on how long his supplies would last told me, well, it's just implausible for his supplies to last long enough. So that's a simple case where science creates plot. Then he needs to have this much water to grow food. He can get plenty of dirt from outside, but he needs the dirt to have a certain amount of water. I did all the math to figure out how much water he'd need, and it was just implausible that a manned mission would carry that much water."

Weir, through Watney, does more than just detail the science of Martian exploration. His book explicitly uses prior, real world missions, such as Pathfinder, to further its plot and play a key role in the story. *The Martian,* in many ways, is about as far as one could go from the earliest conceptions of Mars, and borrows extensively from real-world knowledge: Mars is a dry, uninhabitable location in the solar system, far from a destination to settle on or to meet strange Martians. Other recent Mars books, such as Greg Bear's *War Dogs,* which sets an interstellar war on the surface, highlights the real focus on life support and survival on an inhospitable surface.

When asked about what attracts us to Mars, Kim Stanley Robinson highlighted our growing and changing understanding of the planet:

"Throughout human history it's been interesting because it's red, it gets brighter then dimmer, and it has a hitch in its motion, going retrograde against the stars for a while. Then when we learned it was a planet, the next one out from us, we very quickly saw the polar ice caps, and the changing color, which looked seasonal. It seemed like it could be like Earth. Then Percival Lowell set everyone's imagination on fire with his idea that he was seeing a system of canals, which meant a civilization and possibly aliens like us. Through the decades since there have been repeated alterations in the scientific explanation of the planet's physical situation, which gave science fiction writers new scenarios for stories. Then the Mariner and Viking orbiters and the Viking landers gave us the real landscape, and it was extremely interesting, and to an extent, Earthlike. The idea of terraforming Mars quickly followed."

Mars, for as long as it will hang in the skies above, will continue to inspire authors and astronomers alike, long after we visit, settle and give the planet a new name: Home.

ABOUT THE AUTHOR

Andrew Liptak is a freelance writer and historian from Vermont. He is a 2014 graduate of the Launch Pad Astronomy Workshop, and has written for such places as *Armchair General, io9, Kirkus Reviews, Lightspeed Magazine,* and others. His first book, *War Stories: New Military Science Fiction* is now out from Apex Publications, and his next, *The Future Machine: The Writers, Editors and Readers who Build Science Fiction* is forthcoming from Jurassic London in 2015.

Neither Here Nor There:
A Conversation with Cat Rambo
ALVARO ZINOS-AMARO

I first discovered Cat Rambo's work with the tightly coiled "Worm Within," which got under my skin in a serious way. Ever since then I've kept an eye out for her remarkable stories, and I'm sure that over the years—my reality-bound ophthalmologist to the contrary—this has enhanced if not my vision then at the very least my sense of perspective.

These days whenever I'm at conventions I make it a point to attend whatever writing-related panels Cat is on, as she's a veritable fount of useful, experience-based advice, always leavened with humor. Somewhat surprisingly, the conversation below was our first lengthy exchange.

Cat Rambo lives and writes in the Pacific Northwest, with occasional peregrinations elsewhere. A World Fantasy Award and Nebula nominee, she has 200+ fiction publications, which have appeared in *Asimov's, Tor. com,* and *Clarkesworld,* as well as in audio form and a dozen different languages. She is the current Vice President of the Science Fiction and Fantasy Writers of America. Check her website for links to her fiction and information about her popular online classes.

You've been publishing short fiction prolifically since around 2005 and Beasts of Tabat, just released, is your debut novel. Did you see yourself as going through some kind of craft apprenticeship by writing those 200+ short stories, a way of building up to a novel, or was it not planned that way?

It wasn't planned that way at all. My plan was to get out of Clarion West in 2005 and write a just absolutely killer novel that would set the world afire. But while I was at Clarion West, every once in a while someone would say to us, "Some of you won't write after the class." Or, "Some of you will be so busy processing that you'll be totally blocked for months." And worse, "Some people never write again." My response was pretty much, "Fuck that!"

I came out of Clarion completely determined not to do that and I started a novel immediately. For two months after Clarion West I also made myself write a short story a week, and one of the things I'd learned is that you send stuff out, so I would send the stories out. I kept working on the novel, and some of the stories hit. A year and a half went by and I was still working on the novel and my husband said, "Do you think possibly you may need to put that aside for a while and work on something else?" I was just beating my head against this thing. So I did write something else, and then came back to the novel, and so on. I've been working on *Beasts of Tabat* in one form or another since 2005!

Those forms have been very different. An early version of the book, for example, was set in the school that is featured in *Beasts of Tabat,* the Brides of Steel, but it involved two of the students, because at the time I was thinking in terms of YA. And then this instructor who was one of the gladiators sort of swaggered in and demanded that the story be *hers*—and that was my introduction to Bella Kanto, who's half of the current book. I may go back and write from the point of view of those two students at some point and pick up that YA story, because even though it's a different plotline I know where it fits into the events of *Beasts of Tabat.*

Most of my Tabat stories do in fact link in to each other. When I was going back to them and also writing this version, thinking of it as the first volume of a quartet, I realized that one of the stories spells out the final arc, another spells out a side character's backstory, and so on. In a sense the prewritten stories—and the ones yet to be written—are like a fifth, shadow volume to go alongside the quartet of novels.

Speaking of short stories, can you tell us a little about your experiment with Patreon?

I started doing it because my husband and I were going to go on a lengthy road-trip. I had a big backlog of stories because I'm fairly prolific and I didn't want to have to fuss with having to send stuff out while on the road. So I set up a Patreon campaign, and it's been pretty good. I know I can write a story, put it up, people will like it, and I will get money for it, which is really nice.

One reason I'm keeping the Patreon campaign going is that one day I'd like to have my own spec fic magazine, if I can get to the funding levels needed and the Patreon campaign keeps swelling. It may take several years. Or maybe I'll find another route. But I'd really like to do a magazine at some point.

That's exciting. I have to say I loved the design of your collection Near + Far, which has two front covers and can be read starting from either end, like the old Ace doubles. What made you pick that particular design?

I originally had been talking to a friend, Tod McCoy with Hydra House here in Seattle, about publishing with his house. I'd first thought of doing this collection as a two-volume set, because I was in love with little box sets. I thought we could do a tiny box set and it would be really cool, one volume for near future stories, one for far future. Then at some point I was thinking about Ace doubles, and I realized we could not have as many stories but have it as one book that you could open from both sides. I remember thinking at the time that the idea was genius. I called up Tod and said, "I'm a genius! Are you sitting down? This is sooo good, it's going to blow you away!" Two weeks later I'm at the dealer's room at Norwescon and there, of course, is someone who has already done a double-sided book.

I like *Near + Far* because among other things Tod went and looked at hundreds of the old Ace double covers and if you look at it, you can see that he pulled in some of the design elements from those. He really tried to give it that feel.

And we're doing a sequel.

Near + Far *gathered primarily science fiction stories. Will the sequel focus more on fantasy?*

Yes, it's a fantasy companion volume to *Near + Far*. It's called *Neither Here Nor There*. One side is secondary-world fantasy stories, and the other side is fantasy in our own world. We're shooting for a Fall release date; I think it's coming out in October.

I'm really pleased with it. I actually pitched it a couple of years ago, but it took a little while for it to come together. Tod just needs to relax and realize that I'm a genius and he should just do what I like.

Can you tell me a little about your connection with John Barth, who gave you a great blurb when he described your writing as "works of urban mythopoeia"?

When I first went off to grad school, I went to the writing seminars at Johns Hopkins. I was a member of the last graduate class that John Barth taught before he retired. I adored him. He was wonderful. There was a fellowship that I was up for, and what you quoted was part of his recommendation.

I've always liked that blurb very much. It's John Barth! I send him a copy of each of my books and I always get this nice postcard back that says something like, "Well, this is not exactly my cup of tea, but good job!"

How has your work for SFWA influenced your perception of the science fiction community?

I'd learned early on, when I was at Hopkins, that just because someone is a terrific writer that doesn't mean that they're a terrific human being. It's one of those shattering lessons, where you're like, "Oh crap!" It's sometimes sad, when it's somebody whose work you really like.

But the thing I have learned from being at SFWA is that the pay-it-forward ethos is just pervasive in the science fiction and fantasy culture, in a way that is truly amazing to behold. And in my experience it wasn't that way in literary fiction at all. There it was more like, "Here come the new people, let's try to kill them before they get a novel published."

In science fiction I think people are much kinder, much gentler. Of course this is a sort of ironic moment to be saying this, because we're seeing some really horrible, contentious controversies going on right now. I don't really know what to say about all of that, except that I believe, at heart, that fandom is kind and gentle and inclusive. Kindness will prevail.

Talking about the generosity of the field: your various roles within science fiction and fantasy have put you in touch with plenty of up-and-comers. Any new voices you'd like to recommend or single out?

I'm going to point to a number of them. One of them is Usman Malik, who is on the Nebula ballot this year. He came through my class and I already warned him that I would now take credit for everything that he does because he was one of my students. Kristi Charish just published an urban fantasy novel, with more in the pipeline. Jamie Lackey would be another writer to watch. Julia Rios, who is now one of the editors of *Strange Horizons*. I also count her as one of mine—I'm ruthless, once they've come through my class, I claim them forever. When I'm teaching online I see them as little boxes on my screen, but it's always lovely to see them at the cons later.

You edited Fantasy Magazine with Sean Wallace from 2007 to 2011. Did editing take away some of your writing energy?

Oh yeah, definitely. One of the things that was very nice for me when I started working with *Fantasy Magazine* was that Edmund Schubert, who was working on *Intergalactic Medicine Show,* spent some time on the phone with me and said, "You have to realize that the same part of your brain that is the writing part is also the editing part." When I was editing *Fantasy* one of the things I was very clear about in interviews was that I always thought of myself as a writer first. I didn't want to become an editor primarily. Though I enjoy editing greatly, I wanted to be a writer more than an editor. Creating my own stuff is very important to me.

Has editing Fantasy affected how you approach writing your own fantasy stories?

Other than inspiring an irrational hatred of pirates, I think it's made me a better writer because it's made me articulate my philosophy of writing. To give someone good feedback you have to say the belief that you feel they are violating or not violating. Teaching is the same way. In order to explain something you have to understand it. In fact I think teaching is one of the best things for my writing.

You teach close to twenty different classes on all aspects of writing and career management, from how writers can build an online presence to literary techniques for genre fiction, a class out of which was born Rachel Swirsky's Hugo-winning story, "If You Were A Dinosaur, My Love." How do you decide what to teach, and who were some of the teachers that helped you when you were starting out?

I want to clarify that on the spec fic techniques class, Rachel was just sitting in on the class and having fun playing with ideas; I don't know that I have anything to teach Rachel, she's just amazing.

I started teaching writing science fiction and fantasy stories because I was teaching for a local college and I had a lot of people asking me about those particular genres. When Google Hangouts popped up I thought it was cool and started using that.

The reasons I've added classes are because someone has proposed or requested them, or because they're based on classes I've taught before. The class on delivery and description, for example, is one someone had asked me for, but the flash fiction class is based on a class I taught at Hopkins. The literary techniques class is actually one I originally taught as a one-day Clarion West workshop. I test classes, and if there's not a lot of demand for something I tend to drop it off the roster. This April and May I'm teaching a really limited slate, and it's because I knew I wouldn't have much time and I picked my very favorite classes to teach.

Regarding my own teachers: at Clarion West I was lucky enough to have Octavia Butler, Andy Duncan, Connie Willis, Gordon Van Gelder and Michael Swanwick. Amazing people. And after that, I kept taking one-day workshops around here. I took one with Paul Park, one with John Crowley. Karen Joy Fowler also had a fantastic class.

Andy, Connie, and Michael have been very kind in being mentor figures too. Michael in particular I email periodically; I'll say something angst-ridden, and he sort of pats my head and he says, "Go back to writing," and I say, "Thank you." I outsource my anxieties to him and he knows just what to say!

Karen Joy Fowler wrote that your own descriptions are "gorgeous." Fine attention to sensory detail was one of the things that first drew me to your stories. Are you particularly conscious of descriptive passages in your work? Who are some of the authors you feel excel at description?

Yes, I do pay a lot of attention to description. Part of it is that when I was at Hopkins I took a fabulous class that was specifically on description, in which we read Colette, Kawabata, Nabokov and others. We were looking very carefully at individual passages. I still sometimes copy out passages if I really love them.

So who do I love for description right now? Certainly Catherynne M. Valente. She's got that prose that's juicy and beautiful—like eating tangerines. Dorothy Dunnett, who wrote historical fiction. Delany would be another one. I was just looking at *Babel-17* again recently. He manages a page's worth of description in a single line. He's just found that single, beautiful detail; it's like a fractal, and everything crystallizes out from it.

The Beasts of Tabat is the first in a projected quartet. Why four novels rather than, for example, a trilogy? Do you know how the overall story ends? How much planning did you do before you sat down to write the first novel?

Originally I did think it would be a trilogy. A lot of people write fantasy trilogies, after all. But then I realized there was too much stuff I wanted to cover, and the structure that I wanted to do didn't work with a trilogy. The structure is an odd one: the second book starts midway through the first book, and follows two different characters throughout the entire book, and then the third book starts in the middle of that book, and then the fourth book is going to be this cavalcade of stuff.

The fourth book, *Gods of Tabat,* isn't written but I do know what's going to happen. I know the overall plotline, I know certain moments, and I know pretty much what will happen to each major character. There's a lot of side characters I'm still not sure about, in terms of where they'll be. Book three, *Exiles in Tabat,* is an inchoate mass right now. Book two, *Hearts of Tabat,* is pretty much totally plotted and about half-way written. I hope to turn it in by July. This is one of the advantages of being with a small press; we could actually see volume two out this year. That could make for a great publishing schedule. It's satisfying and a little frightening at the same time.

Were there previous attempts at novel-writing?

Yes, there were several. My first was a YA story. It's about a heroine who is this reluctant champion of Faerie and also just happens to be a little chubby. People keep getting bitchy about it and she says, "Screw you. This is who I am." My first agent shopped it around and no one wanted to buy it. I do want to go back and rewrite it one day—I suspect I've learned enough things that I could make it more sellable now. Then I gave my agent a different book, a paranormal romance, and she shopped that around and no one wanted to buy it either. I'm kind of glad it wasn't picked up because I'm not very happy with it.

I also started writing an urban fantasy called *The Easter Bunny Must Die*, with a world a little like the world of *Who Framed Roger Rabbit*? I got halfway through that and will probably go back and finish it at some point.

With *Beasts of Tabat*, I'm conscious that this is the sort of book I'd like to be known for. I'd like to think it's a good, interesting fantasy novel, and has some serious stuff at its heart too.

ABOUT THE AUTHOR

Alvaro Zinos-Amaro is the co-author, with Robert Silverberg, of *When the Blue Shift Comes,* which received a starred review from *Library Journal.* Alvaro's short fiction and poetry have appeared or are forthcoming in *Analog, Nature, Galaxy's Edge, Apex* and other venues, and Alvaro was nominated for the 2013 Rhysling Award. Alvaro's reviews, critical essays and interviews have appeared in *The Los Angeles Review of Books, Strange Horizons, SF Signal, The New York Review of Science Fiction, Foundation,* and other markets. Alvaro currently edits the blog for *Locus.*

Another Word:
It's Good to Be Lazy and Foolish
KEN LIU

I've been employed in three professions that all involve working with a lot of text: programming, law, and creative writing. I'd like to show you what I've learned from the first two that I think can be helpful to writers.

Among software developers, there's a generally accepted belief that the most productive programmers are lazy and dumb.

What?

Okay, allow me to explain. Laziness is a virtue among programmers because lazy programmers are interested in doing their jobs in a way that *maximizes* using the *creative* parts of their brains and *minimizes tasks* that are better left to the machine.

Here's an example.

Programmers are often faced with the need to modify text across many lines across multiple files in some systematic manner. This could be because of a change in the interface definition of a module (e.g. all instances of *GreatLibrary_procedure()* now have to be changed to *AwesomeLibrary_function()*), because of a change in coding style or naming convention (so all instances of *AwsomeLibrary_function()* have to be changed to *awesome_library_function()*), or because of some quirk of the syntax of the language (e.g., in Python, indentation of lines is important for control flow, so frequently blocks of code have to be indented or unindented as a unit).

Text editors used by programmers are optimized to make many of these systematic changes easier, though one often has to learn arcane commands for how to invoke these capabilities (just look up *vi* and *emacs*). A programmer who is *not* lazy, who is focused on getting the job done and meeting the daily lines-of-code metric, will learn the minimum amount necessary, open up the files, and get to work. If that means pushing the tab key at the beginning of each line twenty times, or opening every file in a directory of three hundred and running the same search-and-replace sequence one by one, so be it. Two hours later, the changes are still not complete, and the programmer is suffering from carpal tunnel syndrome—and by the way, they missed a couple of files in this tedious process. But to the inexperienced manager, it seems the programmer is working hard.

The lazy programmer, on the other hand, will seem to hardly be working in the interim. They spend the time to learn the text editor. They study its commands and syntax and scripting language and support for regular expressions until they can wield it like a robotic servant. This process might take hours. But when they're done, they'll write a few lines of magical incantation, and voilà, all three hundred files will be changed perfectly and instantaneously.

The sort of laziness I'm praising, in other words, is an aversion for drudgery. It might be quicker in the short term to push the tab key twenty times in a row, but it's more *fun* to learn how to use the macro system to accomplish the same thing in three or four keystrokes. Instead of copying-and-pasting a block of code, they'd rather refactor that into a separate function. Instead of extending and elaborating on a bad foundation, they prefer to rewrite the system from scratch so it's more solid. Instead of doing things the way it has always been done, they prefer to find a more elegant and beautiful shortcut. Thus, they invest the time into intellectually stimulating tasks that may (or may not) pay off later, even if that means they won't write the lines of code demanded of them that day.

So what about "dumb?" Rather than keep on using that word, which is probably outdated, I prefer to think of the quality I'm praising as "foolishness," in the sense of "stay hungry, stay foolish." This is related to the aversion of drudgery. Foolish programmers know that they're not the best at their job and believe that there is probably a better way.

The foolishness that I'm praising is related to this aversion of drudgery. These types of programmers know that they're not the best at their job and believe that there is probably a better way. They're curious about new text editors, new programming languages, new design patterns, etc., because they think someone smarter has invented a way to do the job better, a way that they can adopt so that they can be even lazier.

When I became a lawyer, however, I found out that the way the profession approached text was very different (caveat, I'm obviously talking from my very limited experience in corporate law, and I must note that I generally had very positive experiences with my mentors). Lawyers seem intent on treating contracts as a patchwork of magical phrases that must be preserved *exactly as they are*, and laziness is actively discouraged. For example, if some complicated clause drafted with the typical pleonastic legalese ("sell, convey, license, lease, rent, assign, or otherwise transfer") is needed multiple times in a contract—perhaps with minor variations—then the safe thing to do is to copy and paste that language everywhere and adapt as necessary, instead of refactoring into something more elegant. And if that means a great deal of drudgery for the associates and legal secretaries, that's even better, because lawyers are paid by the billable hour.

To some degree, this is understandable, as lawyers live in perpetual fear that changing a single word in some well-worn bit of legalese will cause a judge to suddenly decide to give the clause a new interpretation. Besides, every lawyer lives in mortal fear of admitting that they don't know something, and so being foolish is not even an option—the words from the form document must remain exactly as they are because they contain magic. Thus, refactoring is out, as is any attempt to make things more elegant and concise. When in doubt, just add more words and clauses to dangle from a rickety, unstable framework until contracts turn into messy, ridiculous structures full of hoarded junk that hasn't been touched since the 18th century. But hey, that means even more copying-and-pasting and proofreading and reference checking and modifying for subject-verb agreement . . . and more billable hours!

I think writers should think more like programmers and less like lawyers. Instead of striving hard to meet some daily word count goal, I advocate giving yourself permission to be lazy. It's fine to spend the time to work out worldbuilding details that will never go into the finished story because it's intellectually stimulating and fun. It's fine to think about how to accomplish characterization and worldbuiding, and advancing the plot all in the same scene, even if that means you end up writing fewer words that day. It's fine to throw away a draft and start a new story from scratch if continuing to work on the flawed draft feels like drudgery and deprives you of joy. It's more than fine to refuse to do the same thing you've done many times (and may have found success with) because it now feels tedious—better to be lazy and think of something new to try.

And it's perfectly valid for writers to admit that they are foolish, that they don't know what they're doing. Such an attitude leaves one open to influences from everywhere, not just the *right* critiques or the *best* books. If you see a story resonating with readers but doing things in an unusual way, try to understand why it works. If you see writers succeed by following a different career path than you've envisioned for yourself, try to see if they have lessons to teach you. If you hear advice that is counterintuitive or sounds dumb, try to resist the urge to dismiss it out of hand and see if there is, in fact, something in it that you can learn.

Above all, don't be like the lawyers who treat template contracts as sacred spells that must be preserved at all costs. Writing is a kind of magic, but it's the living magic of making a connection between the reader's mind and yours, not the dead magic of judges' interpretations. Take risks; leave out things that "everyone" claims you must have; add in things that "no one" thinks will work; experiment; mix it up; rewrite the rules if you don't like them; tell, if you don't believe it should be shown; dare to boldly stick in that adverb, write the story that only you can write.

ABOUT THE AUTHOR

Ken Liu is an author and translator of speculative fiction, as well as a lawyer and programmer. A winner of the Nebula, Hugo, and World Fantasy Awards, he has been published in *The Magazine of Fantasy & Science Fiction, Asimov's, Analog, Clarkesworld, Lightspeed,* and *Strange Horizons,* among other places. He lives with his family near Boston, Massachusetts.

Ken's debut novel, *The Grace of Kings,* the first in a silkpunk epic fantasy series, will be published by Saga Press, Simon & Schuster's new genre fiction imprint, in April 2015. Saga will also publish a collection of his short stories.

Editor's Desk:
Overload!
NEIL CLARKE

Spring is finally here in NJ and I can once again bear to go outside. For a while there, it seemed like the winter would never end. I spent a lot of time by the fireplace working on a variety of projects and it's only come to my attention today that I neglected to tell you about one of them. Sometime in 2016, Night Shade Books will be publishing my first year's best anthology: *The Best Science Fiction of the Year, Volume 1.*

As a short fiction aficionado this promises to be a lot of fun and more than a little intimidating. I already read a lot of stories, but now that pile has grown significantly. It walloped me even more when I realized that the last editor to use this title was Terry Carr. I have those books on my shelf and they were a regular part of my annual reading for a long time. No, no pressure there.

It's a complete coincidence that I launched *Forever Magazine* earlier this year, however. If the book deal came in just a bit sooner, I might have delayed that one a bit, but in retrospect, a reprint magazine makes a great companion project for a year's best series. It might also give people an early impression of what that series will be like as my tastes run a bit broader than I might normally consider right for *Clarkesworld*. Do I have you interested? Good. Check out forever-magazine.com for more details or subscribe via Amazon, Weightless, or B&N (soon).

If that isn't enough, I'm also well into the planning stages for my next original anthology. I'm not sharing any details yet as I haven't decided whether or not I should pitch this to a publisher or handle it myself. There is a certain attraction to having someone else handle publication, particularly since I'm juggling all these projects on a part-time basis. That said, I make more going the direct route and that might just help me move towards full-time.

Decisions. Decisions.

I should probably get back to work now.

ABOUT THE AUTHOR

Neil Clarke is the editor of *Clarkesworld Magazine,* owner of Wyrm Publishing and a three-time Hugo Award Nominee for Best Editor (short form). He currently lives in NJ with his wife and two children.

Cover Art:
Io Emissary

JULIE DILLON

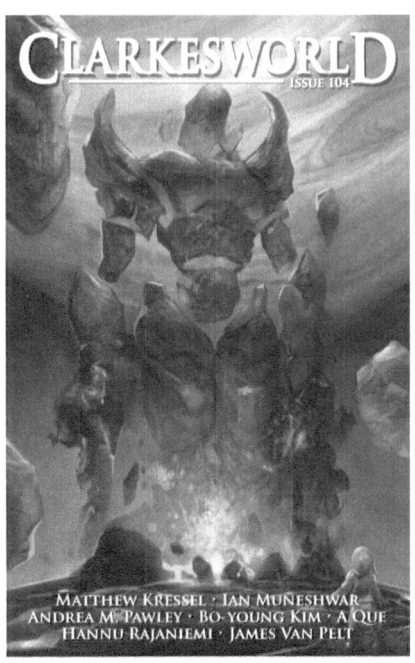

Julie Dillon is a science fiction and fantasy illustrator creating art for books and magazines, as well as for her own projects and publications. She has won two Chesley awards, a Hugo Award, and has been nominated for two World Fantasy Awards.

WEBSITE

juliedillonart.com